PERFECT CATCH

A Baseball Romance Novel

Christy Ryan

CR Dixie Publishing © 2018

ACKNOWLEDGEMENT

Thank you to my friends and family who have stood by me as I took a leap of faith and left an eighteen-year career in education to pursue my dream of writing. Thank you for all those who encouraged me to continue when times and finances got tough. Thank you to my two boys, Wesley and Spencer, who had to put up with me as I worked to complete this book and pursue a new career. Most importantly, thank you to God for the skills, the ability and my love of writing.

"Life will always throw you curves, just keep fouling them off...the right pitch will come, but when it does, be prepared to run the bases."

-      Rick Maksian

PROLOGUE

"This is amazing," McKenzie Harper stated as she and Marcus Hunter strolled onto the roof top of the old Sears Building in Atlanta. The rooftop had been transferred into a park with a few carnival games, mini-golf, a slide, a restaurant and an amazing view of the city.

She glanced over to Marcus who was dressed in a pair of distressed jeans and a navy button down shirt with the top button undone. His sleeves were rolled up displaying the tattoo on his forearm of 3 simple arrows pointing down toward his hands. She had never noticed it before and wondered if they were new.

McKenzie was unsure about coming to the party. She had come up to visit her niece, Josie, who had been born a week earlier. Her brother in-law, Braxton Millican, was the starting pitcher for the Atlanta Eagles MLB team and the owner was throwing a Christmas party at Skyline Park for the players, coaches and staff. Since Josie was only a week old, her sister, Kendall and Braxton, had decided it would be best to forego the party tonight.

The Atlanta Eagles baseball team always went down to Orlando for spring training. During that time, Marcus, the catcher, and McKenzie had gotten to know each other. They had even taken her nephew, Jaxson, to Disney together. Between all their bickering and playful banter everyone expected the two of them to get together, but despite Marcus's best efforts nothing had happened between them.

A month ago, Marcus was down in Orlando as a witness in the trial against Kendall's ex-boyfriend, Chase McIntyre. He had done several illegal things including kidnapping her to try and win her back. After the trial was over, Marcus talked McKenzie into coming up to Atlanta and being his date for tonight's party. While she teasingly complained that it was a long way for a date, he had used the birth of her niece as a way to get her up there.

"I thought you would enjoy it," Marcus admitted as he took McKenzie's hand and intertwined his fingers with hers. As much as she hated to admit it, she loved holding his hand. She loved feeling his callous baseball hands holding her soft hands. As much as she teased him, she went through several outfits trying to decide what to wear tonight. She finally decided on a pair of skinny jeans and a form fitting off the shoulder red sweater and a pair of black high heeled boots which came just below the knee cap. From the expression on Marcus' faced when she answered the door at Braxton and Kendall's house, she had chosen the right outfit.

"Hey, McKenzie!" Tex Jamison, the short stop, came up and gave her a hug. "You finally got her up here," he turned and looked at Marcus with a grin across his face.

"Yeah." Marcus smiled. "Now, let go of my date."

Tex winked at McKenzie and then slowly released her. "About time you got up here, it's not the same without you and Marcus ragging each other all the time," Tex laughed as a tall blonde walked up to him and wrapped her hands around his left arm.

"Tex, Baby, are you coming?" she whined.

"In a minute. Can you go grab me a beer?" Tex asked her and shooed her off.

"Who's the blonde?" McKenzie inquired.

"Um, Callie, Cassie, Carla, I honestly can't remember her name. She's just some baseball groupie," he smirked as McKenzie gave him a weird look. "Don't look at me like that, you turned down all my advances for his ass," he laughed pointing at Marcus. "I had to come up with a date for tonight."

"Come on, let's go get something to drink," Marcus responded as he possessively wrapped his arm around McKenzie's waist.

After a few drinks and some appetizers, Marcus led McKenzie over to the mini golf section of the rooftop. Tex and his date, Callie, joined them.

"Let me show you how this is done." Marcus flashed his pearly whites as he took a swing and completely missed it. McKenzie laughed so hard she could barely contain herself.

"That's how it's done, huh? Man, all these years and I've been doing it all wrong." McKenzie smirked as she walked up, took a swing and made a whole in one.

"Show off," he grinned as he wrapped his arms around her waist and kissed her neck. "You know I was supposed to get another hit, right?"

"I'm impatient, I couldn't wait any longer," she seductively teased him as she got close up and whispered in his ear. He moaned as McKenzie looked and saw him adjusting himself. She laughed inwardly that secretly likes that she could do that to him.

Callie was next up to hit. She grumbled when she missed, blamed Tex for being in the way and then talked about how she was going to mess up her nice manicure. Tex rolled his eyes as he took his place and got ready to swing. McKenzie walked off to the side and Callie followed.

"Marcus sure seems to like you," Callie observed.

"Yeah." McKenzie kept it short and sweet.

"He's a good catch. Hold on to him. I'm hoping things work out with Tex." She smiled and waved at him, "If we can land these two, we'll be set for life girl," Callie started talking to McKenzie like they were best friends."

"If you're trying to win Tex over, you probably shouldn't complain about everything," McKenzie stated, "just a thought."

"Oh, he'll forget all about the complaining to-night when we get home," she winked, "You know you've got to give some to get," she continued. "I plan on giving Tex the best night of his life tonight, one he won't ever be able to forget. He'll want me in his life forever," she chuckled. "Can you imagine telling everyone you are married to an MLB player? On top of that, you wouldn't have to work anymore. Not to mention all the prestige that comes with it."

"That sounds good and all, but what about the ten months they are away paying baseball. Won't that be hard on you?" McKenzie asked.

"There are other men around to keep us company during that time, you know they'll be doing the same on the road."

"You don't want someone who loves you and

only you?"

"No, I just need some eye candy that can take care of me." She smiled looking at Tex, "and he's definitely eye candy."

"Oh, I see," McKenzie said as she looked down and began playing with her phone. She looked over at Tex who was looking at his phone laughing. She figured he had just gotten the text she had sent him.

McKenzie: Ditch the bitch.

Tex: I was planning on it.

McKenzie: I'd do it sooner rather than later. I have a feeling that pussy has seen a lot of action.

Tex laughed again, nodded and put the phone in his pocket. She smiled and put her phone in her pocket as she glanced over to Callie who was taking selfies and not paying attention to anything going on around her.

Even though McKenzie's feelings for Marcus were strong, her and Tex had grown close to each other this past season. She loved Tex like a brother and would not let some hussy like Callie get a hold of him. She would talk to Kendall and see if they couldn't come up with someone who would be good for Tex. Her best friend Piper popped into her mind. She loved baseball, although she was a Miami fan, but she wouldn't date someone because of their job. Maybe she could introduce them to each other when the team came down for spring training.

Hours later, the party was winding down when Marcus suggested to some of the guys and their dates that they come back to his place. He wasn't ready to let McKenzie go, but he didn't think she would go back to his place alone, so he concocted a plan to have some of the players over. After the last of his friends left at 2:00 AM, McKenzie sat on the couch looking at him.

"You want me to take you back to Kendall's house now?" Marcus said sitting down beside her placing his hand on the back of her neck and rubbing it.

"Probably should," she leaned into him as he moved his arm from around her neck and wrapped it around her shoulders.

"It's late, you could stay here, I have a guest room you could stay in," he offered, "or you could stay in my room with me."

"Presumptuous, aren't we?"

"More like hopeful," he leaned over and kissed her gently on the lips before leaning back into the sofa.

"You know this is a bad idea, right?" McKenzie then leaned up and over then kissed him gently before sitting back down and leaning back against the sofa.

"Oh, yeah," he responded as he sat back up and then leaned over and kissed her more intensely this time.

"Marcus?" she continued to kiss him.

"Yeah, Baby?" he came up for a breath as he continued kissing her.

"What are we doing?" She asked breathlessly.

"Kissing."

"You know what I mean," she popped him on his chest. He grabbed her hand and held it tight, before pulling her up and onto his lap.

"Something we've both been fighting for way too long." He pulled her closer to him and crashed his lips on her, as he quickly moved his hands down to the hem of her shirt and instantaneously removed it.

In return, McKenzie hastily reached for the hem of his shirt and lifted it up over his head. He sat up slightly to allow the shirt to come off. He then gathered her in his hands and stood up. She wrapped her legs around his waist. Marcus got a good grasp of her ass and carried her back to his room without removing his lips form hers.

They spent the evening making love over and over again. They both knew things between them would be different from here on out, but how was yet to be seen.

CHAPTER ONE

Marcus walked up to McKenzie's apartment. It had been two months since he had seen her. The night they spent together after his work Christmas party was magical, but she had to return back to Orlando and back to work. They had talked on the phone several times since then, but it wasn't the same. Spring training started in a week, so Marcus decided to come down early to spend time with her before the practices and games started.

He was a little nervous as he walked up to her apartment. He hadn't told McKenzie he was coming, and he hoped she would be happy to see him. They had a magical night together, but at this point, that's all it had been. While he wanted it to be more than a one-night stand, he knew that it very well could be just that. Even the conversations they had were more banter than flirtatious. They had not made a commitment to one another, so he very well knew she could be seeing someone else as much as he hated that idea.

Marcus knocked on the door and waited. At first no one came to the door, he listened for a minute, but didn't hear anything. Just as he started to knock again, he heard a noise inside and then the door unlocking. The door slowly unlocked and there stood McKenzie right before him. She was wearing a ratty old t-shirt, and a pair of sweatpants. Her hair was disheveled, and her eyes were red, swollen and puffy.

"Baby, what's wrong?" Marcus stepped in to gather her in his arms, but she stepped back from him, then pulled out her hand from behind her back. In her hand she was holding a white stick. Marcus knew exactly what it was as he took it from her. Staring at the stick he saw two pink lines and then looked at her, "positive?"

She nodded her head. He stepped into her apartment, shut the door with his foot, grabbed her and wrapped his arms around her, while he tried to wrap his mind around what was happening.

"Come on, let's sit down," he led her to the couch. She sat down with him and laid in his arms as he wrapped his arm tightly around her. "I don't want this to come off as me sounding like an ass, but is it mine?"

"Yes, ass, it's yours!" McKenzie slapped him on the chest and then pulled away from him.

"I'm sorry, Baby," we just haven't seen each other in two months, never said anything about being exclusive, I just had to ask. Forgive me?" He said, pulling her back into him and giving her a kiss on the top of her head. "Well, shit!"

"Yeah, shit's right," McKenzie responded.

"Let's not panic yet, I mean sometimes these things can be wrong." Marcus tried to remain calm.

McKenzie looked at him, rolled her eyes and then stood up and walked out of the room.

"Shit!" Marcus whispered to himself as he stood up and followed her, "McKenzie," he hollered as he followed her into her room. He froze as he walked in and saw what looked to be ten more pregnancy tests sitting on her dresser.

"Not a false pregnancy," McKenzie retorted.

"Nice thought though."

"Fuck," he ran his hands through his hair.

"You can go now."

"No, I'm not going anywhere."

"Just go!" She hollered as she pushed his chest to get him to move.

He didn't budge, just grabbed her wrists. He then took both of her small petite hands in one of his big hands and lifted her chin with his other hand. "Kenz, I am not going anywhere. We are going to work this out together. Just give me a minute to process all this." He stepped back and looked at her. "When was the last time you ate something?"

"I don't know, I throw up most everything I eat anyway," she replied.

"Why don't I order a pizza. Maybe you can get a little something in your stomach."

"Plain cheese," she responded. "I can't even handle the smell of meat, let alone eat it."

"Okay, plain cheese it is. I'll get you a Ginger Ale too. That's what my mother use to give me when I was little, and I had an upset stomach. Maybe it'll help."

"Okay."

"Why don't you go take a shower, while I order the pizza. You look like shit."

"Thanks," she said sarcastically as she headed toward the bathroom.

A little while later, Marcus walked back in the bedroom to check on McKenzie. She had taken her shower and was sitting on the bed in just a towel. She was sitting up against the headboard with her knees drawn up to her. Her hands were wrapped around her knees and her face was buried in them. Marcus couldn't hear her but could tell by the way her body moved up and down that she was crying. He walked over to her and sat on the bed beside her. He put his arm around her and pulled her toward him. She started sobbing as he held her tight. Neither saying a word.

Twenty minutes later, the doorbell rang. Marcus reluctantly pulled away from her. "Pizza's here. Get dressed meet me in the living room, well eat something and see what we can figure out."

McKenzie just nodded her head. Marcus leaned over and kissed her on top of her head before he went to get the pizza and pay the delivery man.

When McKenzie came into the living room, Marcus had already laid out the box of pizza and two plates on the coffee table, he also had a glass of ice next to a bottle of Ginger Ale for her and had grabbed a beer from her refrigerator for himself.

"Guess I should get rid of the beer now." She commented looking over at Marcus' drink.

"Nah, you can leave them here for me or I can take them if you think you'll be tempted."

"I'll be fine with them here."

"Okay. Eat," Marcus commanded.

McKenzie looked at him, picked up a slice of pizza and ripped off a slice in her mouth as she stared him down.

"Good, girl," Marcus smirked.

"Thanks, Dad," she responded sarcastically. However, right after she said it, she stopped chewing and looked at Marcus, he was staring straight at her with a blank look on his face."

"I'm going to be a dad," he finally spoke up. "I'm responsible for another human being."

"We're responsible for another human being." McKenzie corrected him.

"Yeah, we're," he ran his fingers through his hair again.

McKenzie looked at him and snorted.

"What?" He asked looking at her.

"Do you realize, every time you get nervous or frustrated you run your hand through your hair?"

"No, I don't."

"Yeah, you do."

"Really?"

"Yeah, really."

"Huh," he puffed.

"Marcus?"

"Yeah, Kenz."

"What are we going do?"

"I don't know, but we'll figure it out."

"How? I'm here in Orlando. You're here for what 6 weeks maybe and then in Atlanta. Only you're not really in Atlanta because you travel all the time, so there is no every other weekend thing going on."

"Every other weekend? Like in shared custody?"

"Yeah."

"No, we're not doing that."

"Then what are we going to do?"

"I don't know, but we'll figure it out. We don't have to figure it out today. We have nine months."

"Seven," she responded.

"What?" Marcus glanced at her quizzically.

"Seven months, I figure I got pregnant the night of the Christmas party and that was about two months ago, so nine minus two equals seven. Seven months."

"Okay, smartass, seven months." Marcus cracked the first smile since he had gotten there.

The two of them spent the rest of the night making small talk. He held McKenzie tight while they talked. At times she would break down and Marcus would just hold her and let her cry, then she would pull herself back together. Eventually, she fell asleep on him. He slowly picked her up and took her back to her bedroom, laying her gently on her bed. He covered her up with a blanket then left, locking the door behind him and vowing he would be back tomorrow.

CHAPTER TWO

Marcus woke up the next day with a hangover. After leaving McKenzie's apartment late last night, he came home and drank one beer after another. He slowly made his way into the living room and looked over at the coffee table. There look to be as many beer bottles on his table as McKenzie had pregnancy tests in her room.

He started walking to the kitchen to make a cup of coffee when he heard a knock at the door. He groaned and slowly made his way over to the door. He glanced at the clock and realized it was almost noon. He hadn't slept that late since he was a teenager.

Opening the door, he saw McKenzie standing there, a little more pulled together than the day before. There she stood, all five feet, two inches of her small frame standing there looking at him. She was wearing a pair of jeans and a form fitting long sleeve t-shirt today, with her hair pulled up in a ponytail. A pair of Vera Wang sunglasses sat on the top of her head.

"Marcus," she finally said as she stood there waiting for him. "You're the one who looks like shit today."

"I'm sorry, I just woke up," he said as he put his hand to his mouth to smell his breath. "Come in."

She slowly walked in and took in her surroundings. As her eyes caught site of the coffee table in the middle of the living room, she turned quickly on him.

"Shit!" Marcus, "Is that what you do when you can't handle things? You get drunk?" she started pacing in the living room. "That's just fucking great, my baby daddy is a fucking alcoholic."

Baby daddy? He thought to himself before spouting off, "first of all, I'm not an alcoholic. I usually do not have more than one or two beers, because I have to stay in shape. Kind of a requirement for my job. Yes, I got I shit faced last night, but give me a break. I just learned my girlfriend was pregnant," he paused for a minute "Oh, wait a minute, maybe I should rephrase that because apparently I'm just the fucking baby daddy!" He shouted out as he ran his hands through his hair. "Fuck!" He barked realizing he did exactly what she called him on yesterday, running his hands through his hair because he was frustrated.

"You're an ass!"

"You didn't seem to mind my ass two months ago, Baby. You know, when we apparently had a fucking one-night stand."

"Fuck you!" McKenzie cried out as she turned and walked out and slammed the door.

"Damn it!" Marcus shouted as he lifted up his coffee table throwing it across the room. All the beer bottles went flying and crashed across the hard wood floor, glass going everywhere.

"Shit!" Marcus fell back into his sofa taking in the scene when he heard a knock at the door. Thinking McKenzie came back, he went to open the door and apologize, "McKen..." He started but then noticed it wasn't her.

"What the hell is going on over here?" Tex asked.

Tex was the short stop for the Atlanta Eagles and one of Marcus' best friends. Marcus, Tex and Braxton Millican, McKenzie's brother-in-law, had been together since the Minor Leagues and as such had formed a strong bond.

Tex had a townhouse right next to Braxton and across from Marcus. They lived in a gated community where several of his team members had townhomes or condos for the spring training season. "I heard yelling over at my place as I was trying to unload the car and then saw McKenzie speeding out of here."

"Shit. Come on in," Marcus responded as he opened his door.

"What the hell happened in here?" Tex demanded as he walked into the living and took in the scene. Broken glass laid all over the floor, the table laid up against the wall next to a larger whole in the wall where the table had obviously hit. Marcus could see anger rising in his friend's eyes and knew exactly what he was thinking.

"I didn't hit her, and I didn't try and scare her. I did this after she left."

"Marcus, what's going on? I've never seen you like this," Tex sighed somewhat relieved that McKenzie had already left.

"McKenzie's pregnant."

"Christmas party?"

"Yeah."

"Wow! Okay, and this is how you handle it?"

"No, I was fine yesterday when she told me. Used a lot of swear words, but other than that, I handled it fine."

"So, explain this," Tex said as he motioned to the

destroyed room.

"I came home last night and started drinking. I was trying to process everything and figure out where we go from here, how we are going to make everything work with her here in Orlando and me in Atlanta for the majority of the year. I started off with one beer and before I knew, I had drunk almost a whole case by myself."

"Go on."

"This morning, I woke up, with a massive hangover I might add, when McKenzie showed up."

"Were you expecting her?"

"No. Hell, I don't even know why she was here. Things went downhill before I even had a chance to figure it out."

"Okay, finish telling me what happened.

"She saw all the beer bottles, called me an alcoholic and then proceeded to call me the baby daddy, just the baby daddy, like I was just some fucking one-night stand that got her pregnant. I care about her, hell I might even love her, and she sees me as just the fucking baby daddy. I just lost it and started yelling."

"Shit, Marcus! Get out of your ass and quit being a pansy little girl, so she called you the baby daddy, big fucking deal. Do you know how many people use that term? In fact, I think I've even heard Kendall say that about Braxton. At least she didn't refer to you as the sperm donor or just a one-night stand." Tex began. "Have you even defined your relationship? Maybe baby daddy is the only way she knows how to define it at this point."

"Damn it! I hadn't really thought about it." Marcus ran his fingers through his hair. "I'm a real ass."

"Yeah, you are." Tex didn't try and sugar coat it. "Listen, go take a shower, pull your shit together. I'll start working on cleaning up in here and you need to go find McKenzie and talk to her."

"Your right. Thanks, Tex." He turned and headed back to his room. He grabbed his phone and sent a quick text before heading into the bathroom.

CHAPTER THREE

McKenzie walked back into her apartment. Her eyes puffy and swollen from all the tears falling down her face. She had never seen Marcus so mad. She was still trying to process what had happened when a text came through.

Marcus: I'm sorry, Baby. I was a complete ass.

She wanted to text back and tell him he was right, he was a complete ass. She also wanted to text him and tell him that she loved him, and she forgave him, but she couldn't. She opted not to respond and let him stew. He was upset that she called him baby daddy, but what else was she supposed to call him. They hadn't defined their relationship, so she didn't feel like she could say boyfriend, and friend was too casual for whatever they had. However, *he* did say girlfriend.

She sat down on the couch and pulled her legs in, unsure of what to do at that point. She had gone over to see him. She didn't really have a reason, she just wanted to be with him, but after everything that happened, maybe she should rethink this with Marcus. Having a child with him was going to be tough, regardless of what happened with them, she would always be connected to Marcus through this child. She didn't think she would be able to handle it if he found someone else and married them and Lord help her if they have kids. Tears started to flow down her face again. *What the hell just happened?*

McKenzie was pulled out of her thoughts as her phone began to ring. Thinking it was Marcus she started to throw it across the room until she saw her sister's name pop up on the phone.

"Kendall," she answered.

"Hey, Kenz. What you are up to?"

"Nothing really?" She said as she tried to control her voice, unsuccessfully.

"McKenzie, what's wrong?"

"Nothing."

"Don't B.S. me. I know when something is wrong, and something is wrong, spill it!" Kendall demanded.

"I'm pregnant." McKenzie let out a deep sigh.

"Wait, what?" Kendall began. "I didn't even know you were seeing anyone. Who's the father?"

"Marcus."

"Oh, wow. When?" She paused, "never mind, it was when you were up her at Christmas time." She stated.

"Yeah."

"Does he know?"

"Yeah."

"McKenzie, you've got to give me more than one-word answers, please. What did he say? What is going on?"

McKenzie began telling her sister everything that had happened last night and then earlier today when she went to Marcus' house to just see him. She told her how he had been drinking the night before, how he went off on her for using the term baby daddy and how angry he was getting. She told her how she left because what she was seeing scared her and finally about the text she had received a little while ago but did not answer.

"You know he will be coming over to talk to you, don't you? Especially if you aren't answering. He realizes he screwed up and he's not going to let it go."

"Damn it, I've got to get out here. Maybe I'll go to Mom and Dad's for a few days. I can't see him right now."

"You know they left this morning for the European tour we gave them for Christmas, right?

"Yeah, I spoke to Mom this morning before they headed out. I don't think Mom and Dad will mind if I go there for a couple of days. He wouldn't think to look for me there, and it will get me away for a few days to think."

"What about work?" Kendall asked.

"We just finished the animated movie, I was telling you about. It comes out in November. You'll have to bring Jax down here, so he can go to the premier with me."

"He'll love that." Jax was Braxton and Kendall's oldest son, McKenzie's nephew. Kendall had hidden the fact that she was pregnant from Braxton and raised Jax by herself until last year when she finally told Braxton. They were able to rekindle their love and became a family with Jax and their newest addition, Josie. "What are you working on now? Will you be able to get away?"

"Yes, I actually have two months off before we begin our next project. I have some odd, end freelance jobs I am doing, but I don't have to go into the office to do them, I can work remotely, so I'll be fine. It'll give me something to do sitting at Mom and Dad's house by myself."

"Okay, we'll it may do you some good to get away, just be careful. If I were you, I'd go ahead and gather my stuff and head out soon. If Marcus is anything like Braxton, I guarantee he will be there within the hour, if not less."

"Okay, guess I need to go and get out of here."

"Call me when you get there so I know you made it safely."

"I will. Thanks, sis." McKenzie hung up the phone and threw it on her counter before heading back to her room to pack. She quickly threw together some clothes into a small suitcase, mainly yoga pants, tank tops and sweatshirts. She didn't feel like she would be going out much. She did, however, throw in a sundress with a sweater and a pair of jeans, just in case she got out. Once she had clothing and toiletries pulled together, she loaded up the things she would need for work.

Grabbing her small rolling suitcase, work bag, purse and her phone off the counter, she headed out of her apartment and to her car. She quickly threw her items in the car and headed toward the back entrance in order to leave. She felt like she would have a better chance of not running into Marcus that way.

She was right, as soon as she started to turn left to go behind the building toward the back entrance, she glanced in the rearview mirror and saw Marcus's Porsche 911 GT3 pull into the parking lot. She recognized his car anywhere. Not a lot of people in her apartment complex drove two hundred thousand-dollar cars.

She took one last glance back, tears welling up in her eyes, drove around the corner and headed out onto the highway toward her parents' home.

CHAPTER FOUR

"Did you talk to her?" Tex asked as Marcus walked up to the bar they had agreed to meet at for dinner.

"No, waited for hours and she never showed. Finally, one of her neighbors said she saw her leaving with her suitcase. I don't know where she went. I called several hotels around to see if she had checked in there, but none of them had anyone registered under her name."

"Think she could've gone somewhere for work?"

"I don't know, I called Braxton to see if he knew anything or if Kendall might know something, but he was at the orthodontics with Jax and said he would call me back after he talked to Kendall."

"Jax is getting braces?"

"Yeah. He's actually excited about it I think."

"Do you think she could have gone to her parents' house?"

"That thought crossed my mind. If I don't find her soon, I'll head out there and check. Of course, then I'll have to deal with her dad and he already hates me. He's going to kill me when he finds out I got his daughter pregnant."

"He got over it with Braxton."

"Yeah, but he had ten years to calm down before Braxton had to face him."

"True," Tex replied just as Marcus' phone began

to ring.

"Hello," Marcus quickly answered the phone.

"McKenzie's pregnant?" the voice from the other end asked.

"Yeah. I'm guessing Kendall talked to McKenzie."

"Yeah."

"McKenzie didn't happen to tell Kendall where she was going, did she?"

"Her parents' house, but you didn't hear that from me."

"Okay. Thanks. Her dad is going to kill me."

"Yeah, he is, but they are not there. They went on that European tour Kendall and I got them for Christmas. McKenzie went down there by herself. She's there and safe. Kendall talked to her not long ago."

"Good, guess I'll head down that way. Can you shoot me the address?"

"Marcus, give her some time before you go down. I'll shoot you the address in a few days."

"Braxton. Come on man, I thought you were my friend."

"I am, and as far as I am concerned your like a brother to me, but McKenzie is family and right now she needs some time to herself."

"Braxton, what if she takes time to think and decides she doesn't need me. I can't leave her there too long to think on her own."

"I don't think she will. She loves you, man. That's why what you did hurt so bad. When you do go, you are going to have to grovel. Take a couple of days and try and figure this out yourself, know what you are going to say to her. Figure out how you can make it work."

"Maybe you are right."

"Of course, I am, but I would also send a few texts each day, even if she doesn't respond. Make it hard for her to try and forget you."

"Okay. Thanks Braxton. When are you heading down?"

"I'll be down Friday. That'll give me the weekend to settle in. I'm getting in as much time as I can with my family before I have to come down."

"I don't blame you. Give everyone a hug for me. See you in a few days." Marcus responded as he hung up and looked over at Tex who was handing him another beer.

"I already had one, I don't know if I need another one."

"Just stop after this one and you'll be fine," Tex drawled. "What did Braxton have to say?"

"She is at her parents' house. He suggested I give her a few days before I go down.

"I think that's a good idea." Tex took a swig of his beer.

"What are you doing down here already? I mean I came early to see McKenzie," Marcus paused, "Guess God had other plans. He's probably up there laughing at me right now."

"Best laid plans," Tex smirked. "I came on down to get settled in and have some down time before we get going."

"Got ya. Let's order. I'm starving, I haven't eaten all day." Marcus waved the waitress over. The entire time she kept trying to get his attention by bending over, her boobs almost falling out of her lowcut shirt and using a sugary sweet tone. At the same time, she laid her hands on his shoulder and arm as she spoke to him. Marcus barely noticed. His mind was on McKenzie and what he needed to do to win her back and be a good father to their child.

◆ ◆ ◆

After several days of moping around and trying to figure out how they could make their relationship work, Marcus was past ready to go see McKenzie. He had tried to keep busy during the day by hanging out with Tex. They played a few rounds of golf and went to the batting cage during the day. They would hang out at night, watching a basketball game or whatever they found on TV.

Braxton had ended up sending McKenzie's parents address the day after they spoke. Instead of jumping in the car and rushing to her, he gave her the time she needed. However, he sent her three text each day, one each morning as soon as he woke up, one in the afternoon and one each evening. She didn't respond, but he kept sending them. However, today was the day he was going to go confront her and talk to her. He had spent a lot of time talking to Tex and talking to Braxton over the phone and had a plan in mind, he knew would work. He just needed to win her back over and he was prepared to grovel in order to do that. He would then explain to her what he had planned and hope she thought it was a good idea too.

Marcus got in his car and headed down the highway toward Vero Beach. He was going a little faster than he should've been, but the hell with it. He wanted to get to McKenzie and he could afford a damn speeding ticket if he got one.

He hadn't gotten too far out of town when he had to slam his breaks on. There was traffic jam on the highway. Marcus looked at his GPS map to see if he could determine if it was construction or an accident. However, as he started moving up he saw flashing blue and red lights. It looked like a firetruck, police car and ambulance. He knew it had to be an accident. As he got closer he saw a large buck dead in the road. Damn deer, he thought. Those things can be dangerous.

As he looked a little closer, his heart stopped, and he felt bile rise in his throat. Down the embankment was a red convertible Chevy Camaro that looked just like McKenzie's. He pulled over quickly to the side of the road and ran over toward the accident. He was stopped by a police officer.

"Whoa, son? Where do you think you're going?" the older police officer asked him.

"That's my girlfriend." He frantically responded.

"Are you sure?"

"I know it is, I recognize her car."

"Son, stay right here. You don't need to go down." He replied sympathetically.

"Is she..." he couldn't bring himself to say it, tears welding up in his eyes.

"She's unconscious, but she's alive. They are trying to get her out, but she's trapped in the car. Let them do their job. They can't take care of her and worry about you too."

"She's pregnant," Marcus told the officer as he ran his hands through his hair.

"Okay. What's her name? "The officer asked.

"McKenzie."

The police officer leaned toward his shoulder and spoke into the walkie attached. "The driver's boyfriend is here, says her name is McKenzie and she is pregnant."

"Roger that," Marcus could see the officer by the car responding and then telling the first responders who were working with her.

Standing at the top of the embankment looking down, Marcus kept wanting to run down there. The officer seemed to know that and took sympathy on him, never saying anything just occasionally putting his hand on his shoulder when he looked like he was about to cave and head down.

Finally, Marcus saw them pulling her out, she had a neck brace around her and an oxygen masks on her face. They gently laid her down on the stretcher which was lying beside the car. He breathed a sigh of relief when he saw her removed from the car but started panicking again as he realized she wasn't moving at all. He knew the officer had told her she was unconscious, but just seeing her like that made the tears that had built up in his eyes start to flow.

"Does she have family close by?" The officer asked putting his hand back on Marcus' shoulder.

"Her parents live in Vero Beach, but they are in Europe right now. Her sister lives in Atlanta, and her brother-in-law is on his way down. We start spring training Monday."

"Spring training, I knew you looked familiar. Marcus Hunter, Atlanta Eagles?"

"Yes, sir."

"Why don't you call your brother-in-law and have him meet you at St. Mary's Hospital. It's not far from here? I'm sure they will need consent from closest of kin and right now, it sounds like that's him."

"Okay. Can I ride with her?"

"Unfortunately, no, only family members are allowed to ride. Besides, I wouldn't want to leave that car of yours out here. There is no telling what will happen to it. You can see her once they get her up here, but they need to get her in and settled quickly and get to the hospital." Once you're ready, I'll stop the cars and let you get turned around and you can follow the ambulance."

"Okay. Thank you," Marcus rubbed his temples.

"Any place particular you want her car towed to once we get it up?

"No, it's totaled. We'll have to get her a new car. I'm thinking a tank."

The officer chuckled and patted his back. "St. Mary's is good. They are going to do everything they can for her and your baby."

"Thanks," he responded as the emergency personnel made their way up the embankment with McKenzie. He walked over to her, put his hand over her head and then leaned over and kissed her forehead. "I love you, Kenz," knowing they had to get her to the hospital quickly, he stepped back and allowed the EMTs to place her in the ambulance. He nodded to the officer that he was ready to get his car turned around.

As he drove his to the hospital he called Braxton on the blue tooth in his car.

"Hello," Braxton answered on the other line.

"Braxton." Marcus barely got his name out.

"Yeah, Marcus, what's going on?"

"How far out are you?"

"About an hour, why? What is going on?" He asked again.

"McKenzie was in an accident. I was heading to her parents' house and come up on it. She's hurt bad. She's unconscious. I'm following the ambulance now, they are taking her to St. Mary's. They said they need the next of kin there to make decisions and since you are her brother-in-law and in the only family member in the state, that's you."

"Shit, next of kin to make decisions?" Braxton, questioned.

"Yeah, I told you it's bad."

"Are you at the hospital now?"

"No, I'm heading that way now, following the ambulance. We are just leaving the scene of the accident."

"Well, shit. Okay, I'm on my way. I'll call my parents and see if they can't take the kids and then call Kendall and get her down here as well."

"Okay."

"Marcus, drive carefully. I'll see you at St. Mary's"

"See you soon," he replied as he hung up the phone.

Marcus kept his eyes on the ambulance in front of him. He knew the image of lights flashing would be engraved in his mind forever. Staring at the lights, his mind started racing to the way he and McKenzie had left things. He just prayed she knew how much he cared about her. One thing for sure, if, no when, she pulled through this, he would not let one day go by without her knowing how much he loved her.

CHAPTER FIVE

Marcus paced back and forth in the waiting room, waiting on any word on McKenzie. The problem was because he wasn't family, they weren't giving him any information.

"Marcus," a voice was heard behind him, coming from the emergency room doors.

"Braxton, thank goodness," Marcus rushed to his friend. "They won't tell me anything, because I'm not a damn relative," Marcus drawled out, "but hell, she's carrying my child. I think the fact that my flesh and blood is inside her body makes me an official relative."

"Calm down, let me go talk to them and see what I can figure out."

Marcus nodded as Braxton turned and walked to the nurses' station. He continued to pace back and forth waiting for Braxton.

"She's going to talk to the doctor and let him know I'm here. I told her I was the closest next of kin and I was giving permission for you to be in the room and get information as well. Hopefully, my permission is good enough. Guess we'll find out soon enough."

"Thanks, man." Marcus said finally taking a seat.

"How are you holding up?"

"Not good," Marcus shook his head. "You should've seen her. She was cut up and blood all over her. You could barely tell it was her."

"I'm so sorry, man. I know how much she means to you."

"Did you get hold of Kendall and her parents?"

"Yeah, I called my parents first to make sure they could take the kids and then called Kendall. My parents are going by the house to pick up Jax and Josie and take them home with them and drop Kendall off at the airport. Tex is going to pick her up at airport."

"Don't you need to be there for her when she gets off the plane. She's going to be upset."

"I had planned on that, but she said she needed me here in case any decisions needed to be made for McKenzie and she felt like I needed to be here for you."

"Here sister is in the hospital and she's thinking of me." Marcus gave a half-grin.

"That's Kendall for you."

"What about her parents?"

"We haven't been able to get hold of them yet. My parents were going to keep on trying, so Kendall could focus on McKenzie and getting here.

"God, Braxton, I can't lose McKenzie." Marcus ran his hands through his hair.

"I know, Kendall won't be able to handle it either." Braxton paused. "We just have to remember that McKenzie is strong, young, and healthy. She'll pull through this."

"You didn't see her. You didn't see her car. They had to use the jaws of life to get her out. She was in a convertible and of course, the top was down." Marcus buried his head into his hands. For the next hour, him and Braxton sat in silence. Marcus heard the door that lead back to the emergency room open and looked up and saw a doctor come out.

"Is the family of McKenzie Harper here?" The doctor asked.

Marcus and Braxton both jumped up and headed toward the doctor.

"You both family?"

"I'm her brother-in-law and right now, I'm her closest living relative. Her sister is in Georgia, catching a flight and heading here as soon as she can. Her parents are overseas, and we are trying to get hold of them. This is her fiancée and father of her child. Braxton explained to the doctor.

"Okay, follow me please." The two of them followed him back to a small room with just some chairs in it. "Take a seat please."

"Where's McKenzie?" Marcus asked.

"She's upstairs in the ICU. We will head that way in a minute. I just wanted to update you on everything before we head up."

Braxton nodded his head and glanced over at Marcus who was barely holding it together.

"First of all, McKenzie is stable. She is in critical condition but is stable for now. We do have her on a ventilator to help her breath. She was breathing on her own, but it was labored. Since we want her to heal as fast as possible, we are using the ventilator to help take some of the pressure off her body. Because she is on the ventilator, we have placed her in a medically induced coma. Our biggest concern right now is the swelling in the brain. We are watching it carefully, if it stays as it is, she will be able to recover on her own. However, if we see any more swelling, we will need to look at surgery."

"Like brain surgery?" Marcus asked.

"Yes." The doctor replied.

Marcus ran his hands through his hair again. "What about the baby?"

"As of right now, the baby is fine. However, with such a traumatic occurrence, the baby is not out of the woods yet. The fact that she is only 9 weeks along, helps a lot, the baby is still well protected."

A relief passed over Marcus' face.

"However, you need to know, if we do end up having to do surgery, the risks of losing your baby increases." The doctor looked at Marcus with sympathy, "not having surgery won't be an option though. If she continues to swell and we don't have the surgery she will die and if she dies, the baby will too because it's not developed enough to live outside of the womb. If she was further along, like twenty-eight weeks, this would be a whole other conversation."

"Anything else we need to know? Anything else I need to tell her sister, when I call?" Braxton asked the doctor.

"Her left leg was broken and a few broken ribs. Those are easy fixes though compared to everything else. It'll be a pain in the butt for her, but they are not life threating. Our focus right now is the swelling in her brain and her just being able to breath on her own."

"You said she was in a medically induced coma. Does that mean she came too at some point? She was unconscious when they pulled her from the wreckage." Marcus asked.

"Yes, she was coming to, but she was fighting us and having a hard time breathing."

"That's good, right?" Braxton inquired.

"Maybe," the doctor replied.

"Can we see her now?" Marcus asked as the tears welded up in his eyes again.

"Yes. Only two people are allowed in the room at a time. I know right now it's just you two, but just keep that in mind as people start to arrive."

"We will. Thank you," Braxton replied as the three of them stood up and headed toward her room in the ICU.

As they got to the room, the doctor stopped and looked at Marcus and Braxton. "Just to warn you, she looks rough," the doctor motioned for them to walk in.

Marcus was the first to walk in, he gasped at the sight in front of him. Rough did not begin to describe her. She had a breathing tube coming from her mouth and several IVs in her hand. She was pale and looked so fragile. He rushed over to her and held her hand. It was cold, which made him shiver. The tears that had been welding up in his eyes began to flow.

Marcus heard the doctor tell Braxton that he would leave them alone for right now, but to push the call button if they needed anything. He then felt Braxton's hand on his shoulder.

"I'm an idiot," Marcus began, "she would have never gone to her parents' house if I hadn't been such a jackass. She would have never been on that damn road if it wasn't for me."

"Marcus, you can't do that. You can't go blaming yourself for this. She is a grown adult and knew what she was doing. No one can predict a deer coming out from nowhere."

"Why did you tell the doctor I was her finance?" Marcus looked up at Braxton.

"Because I felt like they would take you more seriously than just being the boyfriend."

"God, I'm crying like a baby right now," Marcus took a tissue off the side table and wiped his eyes. "There goes my man card."

"If it was Kendall, I would be doing the same." Braxton assured him. "Listen, I'm going to step outside and let her know what is going on and it'll give you some alone time with McKenzie. You going to be okay?"

"Yeah." Marcus confirmed.

As soon as Braxton stepped out of the room, Marcus let go of McKenzie's hand for a minute and pulled a chair up to her bed. "Hey, Kenz," he began, "I don't know if you can hear me or not, but I hope you can. I was a complete ass when you came over. It wasn't because I didn't want the baby. It was because I was hung over and when you called me just the baby daddy, it upset me. I love you, Kenz and I felt like there was more to us then me just being a sperm donor. After you left, and I spoke to Tex, I realized I was a dick. We hadn't defined our relationship and you probably didn't mean anything by it. Kenz, you've got to know you are everything to me and once you and our child pull through this, I am going to do everything in my power to prove it to you. I love you McKenzie," he stood up and leaned over leaving a kiss on her forehead.

Marcus felt a hand on his shoulder, looked up and

saw Braxton standing over him.

"How much did you hear?"

"Not much, just that you are going to prove yourself to her."

"How's Kendall holding up?"

"She's a mess," Braxton responded as he pulled up another chair. She got a flight and should be here by six."

"Braxton," Marcus looked at his friend, "tell me McKenzie is going to make it through this."

"She's going to make it through this. She's a Harper girl., they are not only stubborn as hell, but tough as nails."

CHAPTER SIX

Marcus woke to sobbing and whispering. He hadn't even realized he had fallen asleep, but he had laid his head down next to McKenzie and obviously drifted off. When he lifted his head and looked up, he saw Kendall standing on the other side of bed. Braxton was standing right behind her with his hands on her shoulder.

"Kendall," Marcus said, "you're here. What time is it?"

"It's a little after seven," Braxton responded. You've been asleep for a couple of hours.

"Wow," Marcus shook his head. "How are you doing Kendall?"

"As well as can be expected," she responded as she came over and gave him a hug. "How are you holding up?"

"As well as can be expected," he mimicked Kendall's words.

"She was coming back to you," Kendall stated.

"What?" He looked up at her.

"McKenzie was coming home to you. I talked to her not long before she left. She said she made a mistake leaving, she should have stuck around and tried to work it out or at least talk to you about everything." Kendall told him. "She loves you, you know that, right?"

"She does?" The tears started back in his eyes

again.

"Yes, she told me she did. She was just scared."

"I love her too."

"I know you do, I can see it in your eyes. Kendall responded as the nurse walked into the room.

"Only two people in the room at a time," the nurse responded as she glanced around the room.

"I was just heading out," Braxton stated as he leaned over and kissed Kendall on her cheek. "I'll go keep Tex company in the waiting room. Let me know if you need me." He then looked over at Marcus, "You too."

Marcus moved his chin up to acknowledge his friend and then moved from his chair, so the nurse could check on McKenzie. He walked over to the wall and leaned against it, positioning himself with one leg over the other. Kendall walked over to him and he pulled her in for a hug. She stood their holding onto him, arms wrapped around his lower chest. Neither said anything, just kept an eye on McKenzie and the nurse.

They stood off to the side listening to the nurse as she called the doctor on her phone updating him on her vitals. She then turned and looked at Marcus and Kendall.

"Her blood pressure is elevated. The doctor has ordered a CT scan to check on the swelling."

"How long until the scan?" Marcus asked holding Kendall a little tighter.

"As soon as I can get it set up. It won't take long, you two can wait in here while she's out."

"Okay, thanks," Kendall responded.

It didn't take long for the nurse to reappear with

another nurse in tow. They rolled McKenzie out to have her CT scan. During that time Marcus and Kendall both took restroom breaks and grabbed a snack. They were back in the room before McKenzie was rolled back in. The doctor then came back into the room to talk to the family about what the next steps would be. Even though only two visitors were allowed in at a time, he allowed Braxton to come in while he went over everything.

"The swelling is continuing to put pressure on her brain. We need to do a ventriculostomy, to relieve the intercranial pressure."

"What exactly is a ventriculostomy?" Braxton asked.

"That is where we go in and cut a small hole in her skull," the doctor paused for a minute as Kendall gasped. She was sitting next to Marcus and Braxton was standing next to her. She grabbed hold of Marcus's hand with one hand, Braxton's with the other and squeezed tight as the doctor continued on. "I know that sounds bad, but it is a common procedure. Unfortunately, it's something we have done many times here. I know when it's your sister or your fiancée, it doesn't make it any better," the doctor paused again before continuing. "Most of the time this procedure can be done right at the bedside, but given her fragile state, I would prefer to take her into the operating room. That being said, in a little while I will send in a nurse and she will shave part of McKenzie's head, so I can get to her skull. We have to shave to keep the hair and infections out. I'll then insert a tube which will let the cerebrospinal fluid drain, hopefully, relieving some of the pressure."

"If this doesn't work?" Marcus asked, his voice barely above a whisper.

"Then we look at a Decompressive craniectomy, which is where we remove part of her skull to relieve some of the pressure. However," the doctor quickly began, "I don't think we will need to do that."

"What else do we need to know?" Braxton asked.

"When she comes out of surgery, she will have an EVD, or External Ventricular Drain, attached. We will watch her and determine how long she needs to keep it based on her progress, some only need it for 24 hours, some a couple of weeks. It's a wait and see situation. We will have to keep her at forty-five-degree angle while she sleeps.

"Complications?" Marcus asked.

"There is a small risk of infection or brain hemorrhage. We'll start her on an antibiotic right off the bat to hopefully prevent any infections."

"Our child?" Marcus asked again as Kendall's hand tightened around his and he could feel Braxton's hand on his shoulder.

"The baby is very fragile right now after such a traumatic injury, the risks of lose increases as she goes into surgery. I'm sorry about that, but like we talked about before, the baby cannot live outside of McKenzie, so our focus needs to be one hundred percent on her."

"I agree, I just pray they both make it through," Marcus pulled his hand from Kendall, placed them on his face and leaned down into his knees. He could feel her hand rubbing up and down his back.

"How long will the surgery take?" Kendall asked.

"The procedure itself should take no longer than

thirty to forty-five minutes as long as there are no complications. However, between pre-op, post-op and the actual surgery, it will be two or three hours if not more before you see her again. Post-op, we will want to keep a close eye on her before returning her to the room. During that time, you will need to hang out in the waiting room. Any other questions."

"You'll keep us updated?" Kendall asked.

"Of course," he paused. "If we're good here, I really do need to get her back there, but I need the next of kin signature on some papers to approve surgery. I'll send the nurse in with the paperwork for you to sign," he looked at Kendall.

"Okay," Kendall responded as the doctor stood and left the room. She then looked over at Marcus. "This is what we have to do, right?"

"I don't see where we have an option," he replied, thankful that Kendall was including him in this decision.

The nurse soon came in with the papers. Kendall signed them. She gave her a sister a hug and kiss, telling her how much she loved her and then stepped back. Braxton leaned over and kissed his sister-in-law on the forehead and then stood next to Kendall. Marcus then stood over McKenzie and told her how much he loved her and how he was going to show her every day for the rest of her life how much he did once she pulled through this. He then leaned over and kissed her belly telling 'peanut' to hang on tight and pull through this with his mother.

Next thing Marcus knew, Kendall had her arms wrapped around him with tears flowing down her face. He couldn't help himself as he pulled her in and gave her a tight hug as the tears started flowing down his eyes as well. Braxton walked over and herded them both out of McKenzie's room and to the waiting area, where Tex was sitting waiting on them as well as some of Marcus' other teammates, Jagger, Sawyer and Niko, who shown up to give support.

CHAPTER SEVEN

Marcus paced back and forth in the waiting room for a while before finally sitting down.

"Were you able to get hold your parents, Kendall?" Niko, Marcus' teammate and 3rd baseman asked.

"Yeah, I finally got them as they had touched down in New York. They were going to spend a few days there before heading back home from their cruise, but they managed to get a flight back home sooner. They should be here anytime now.

"Good." Niko responded, but Marcus tensed up even more. He knew Mr. Harper already hated him and was not looking forward to seeing him.

After about an hour, Marcus heard some commotion. He was sitting in a chair with his elbows against his knees his head in his hands. He didn't bother looking up at first but could tell by the voices and what was being said that McKenzie and Kendall's parents had arrived. Braxton and Kendall were trying to update her parents on everything that was going on.

"Come on," he heard Jagger say, "Let's go grab something to eat. Leave the family alone to talk."

Marcus looked up to see Jagger, Sawyer, Niko and Tex heading toward the door.

"Take his sorry ass with you," Mr. Harper said motioning to Marcus. "He's not family."

"I'm not going anywhere," Marcus calmly replied

as the rest of the guys walked on out.

"She wouldn't be in this damn hospital if it wasn't for you. I don't know what happened between you guys. All I know is that she was at my house trying to put distance between you two." Mr. Harper replied.

"She was coming back to me," Marcus tried to remain calm.

"I don't care what she was doing, just get the hell out of here. I don't want to see your ugly face."

"Dad," Kendall started up.

"No, he needs to get the hell out of here, right now, this needs to be just family. He has no right to be here."

"The fucking hell I don't," Marcus finally had enough. "I don't give a fuck what you think about me, but the woman I love is in that operating room fighting for her life as well as my child. As long as she is caring my child, I am fucking family, so shut-up and leave me the hell alone!"

"What the hell!" Mr. Harper shouted, "She's pregnant?"

"Calm down dear," Mrs. Harper spoke up.

"The hell I will, what is it with these fucking baseball players? Do you guys not know how to keep you dick in your pants? Do they not teach you how to use a condom because apparently there needs to be a course in that!"

Marcus looked up at Braxton and Kendall. She had her arm wrapped around Braxton who looked like he was about ready to go off on Mr. Harper as well. Just then a nurse walked into the waiting room.

"I don't know what is going on in here, but the yelling needs to stop, or I'll have to ask you all to leave."

"It'll stop," Mrs. Harper stated matter-of-factly. Sorry for the inconvenience.

The nurse looked satisfied with that and turned around and walked out.

Mrs. Kendall then looked over at her husband, "Now Bill, you know as well as I do that it takes two to get pregnant. I've seen the way McKenzie looks at Marcus and I guarantee you she was a willing participant."

"Kendall," Mr. Harper said looking away from his wife and over to his daughter. "Did you know about this?"

"I just found out this week, but I figured McKenzie needed to be the one to tell you about the baby."

"Well hell," he murmured as he flopped into a chair. Mrs. Harper sat down next to him.

"Look Dad, I don't mean any of this disrespectfully, she walked over to him and leaned down next to him to talk. "I know you're not fond of baseball players, but you have come to love Braxton."

"Tolerate," her dad interrupted.

"Okay," Kendall responded rolling her eyes. "Regardless, Braxton is the best thing that ever happened to me. Without him I wouldn't know what true love is and more importantly I wouldn't have Jax or Josie, both of them come from a baseball player. Can you honestly tell me you think life would be better without them?" He looked at her and shook his head. "I've seen you with them and I know you love them both and there is not a thing you wouldn't do for either of them. I also know that if McKenzie and Marcus' child survives this, you're going to love that child as much as you love Jax and Josie.

"Of course, I will," he responded as Marcus sat and watched in disbelief just how easily Kendall diffused the situation.

"Marcus is good guy Dad," she paused and glanced at Marcus, and he's good for McKenzie. She loves him, and he loves her. If I had any doubt about how much he loved her, after all this, there is not a doubt in my mind. He'll take care of her and he'll do whatever needs to be done to make sure she is happy and well taken care of."

Marcus nodded his head in agreement with Kendall as Mr. Harper glanced over at him.

"How's he going to do that if he's in Atlanta and she's down here?" Mr. Harper asked.

"I'm retiring after this season," Marcus spoke up monotonously.

"What?" Braxton looked over at Marcus.

"Sorry, Braxton," he said apologetically. "I was going to talk to you about this privately before announcing it to everyone, but he's right. I can't be there for McKenzie and in Atlanta at the same time. It's time for me to retire. I'm thirty-six. I've played longer than most MLB catchers. It's time to let some younger players come in. McKenzie's career is really just taking off, she needs to be here, and I want to be here for her and our child. I'm sorry, I know we were going to retire together." Marcus kept his eye on Braxton the whole time, not looking at Mr. Harper who was listening intently.

"Don't apologize. I was going to talk to you at some point, because I'm ready to retire as well. When we talked about retiring in our forties, we were young, single and I don't think either of us thought marriage was in our future. The truth is, I want to be at home with Kendall. I want to watch Josie grow-up," he paused, "and I missed so much of Jax's life, I don't want to miss any more of it. I want to be there for him and help him make his way in this world of baseball."

"Make sure you teach him how to use a condom," Mr. Harper grunted out.

"Dad!" Kendall shouted out.

Before anyone else could respond, the doctor came into the waiting room. He looked over and saw Mr. and Mrs. Harper. "Hi! I'm Doctor Johnston, you must be McKenzie's parents.

"Yes, Bill and Natalie Harper," Mr. Harper held out his hand. The doctor took it and shook his hand.

"Am I free to talk to everyone in here?"

Mr. Harper looked over at Marcus and reluctantly agreed.

"McKenzie is stable and will be back in her room within an hour. We did have some complications. She flatlined at one point." McKenzie's mom gasped as her husband grabbed her hand and squeezed it. The doctor continued. "When she flatlined there was no oxygen getting to her or the baby. We were able to re-suscitate her," he paused and looked at Marcus, "but, unfortunately, we couldn't do anything to save the baby."

Marcus inhaled deeply. Tears he did not know he had, started flowing down his face. Kendall let go of Braxton and went over to Marcus. She sat next to him and grabbed hold of his hand squeezing it tightly. He gave her a quick squeeze back and continued to hold her hand.

"We went ahead and did a D&C while we had her under sedation. In her condition, her body did not need to worry about fighting the miscarriage as well," the doctor paused again before he continued. "Right now, McKenzie is still on a ventilator. Within the next couple of days, we will begin to wean her off, make sure she is able to breathe on her own, without struggling. We will also be checking her to make sure she has no brain damage. Due to her injury, even if she comes through this fine, you may see long term effects later on, such as short-term memory loss, headaches, or even a change in personality. A lot of it is wait and see."

"When can we see her?" Her mother asked.

"We'll let you know when she is back in the room. Once we have her settled in, you can go see her. Just remember only two people at a time."

"Thank you," she replied.

"Keep in mind when you go in there, that she will have the breathing tube and the IVs attached to her. In addition, she will have part of her hair shaved and an EVD catheter coming from her head for drainage.

"How long will she have the catheter?" Mr. Harper asked.

"We will play it by ear, it could be twenty-four hours, could be a couple of days or even weeks." He looked around the room at everyone. "Are there any other questions I can answer?"

"Will she still be able to have kids?" Marcus asked.

"Yes, miscarriages are common, unfortunately. While hers was caused by a traumatic event, it should not affect her ability to get pregnant and carry a child full term in the future."

Mr. Harper glared at Marcus, Kendall noticed it and spoke up, "I'm glad you asked him that, McKenzie will want to know that once she gets through the emotional turmoil she's about to go through."

"I'm going to head back to the post-op room and check on her. I'll send a nurse to let you know when she's back in her room." The doctor responded as he stood up and headed out of the waiting room.

CHAPTER EIGHT

For the next several days, Marcus stayed at the hospital. The only time he left McKenzie's room was when her parents where there or other visitors had shown up. Braxton had run to Marcus' house and packed him a back with a couple of outfits, toothbrush and toothpaste. Marcus had also talked to the head coach who excused him from reporting to spring training for the time being. He told him to take as much time as he needed.

Currently, he was sitting in the waiting room, again, with McKenzie's parents, Braxton and Kendall. Spring training had officially started, and Braxton had been going to the practices. However, he took today off to be at the hospital with Kendall and Marcus.

The doctor was removing both the EVD and the breathing tube. He was hoping to start bringing her out of her medically induced coma today and test her brain activity. Marcus had spent a lot of time in prayer, just praying that McKenzie would pull through everything okay.

After a couple of hours, the doctor walked into the waiting room. "We removed the EVD and the breathing tube with no complications. She is successfully breathing on her own, so that's good. She also managed to pass the brain activity tests we did, so that's another plus. Once she comes to, we will have a few more tests we will need to do. In the meantime, you can go see her. She does have a bandage around her head where we removed the EVD."

"Thank you doctor," Mr. Harper stood up and held his hand out toward the doctor who took it and shook it.

Mr. and Mrs. Harper were the first to head back to see McKenzie. Marcus did not even attempt to go back. He had decided just to let everyone else go ahead because once he was in her room, he wasn't going to leave.

"Marcus, how are you holding up?" Kendall asked as she came and sat next to him.

"Okay, I guess. I just want her to wake up. Yell at me, mock me, tease me, whatever. I just want to hear her voice."

"I know, me too."

"You talked to her while she was hanging out at her parents, right?"

"Yeah."

"What happened while she was there, what did she do?"

"Nothing really, she worked on some freelance illustrations. She never really left the house other than to grab some groceries. She called and texted a lot, mostly talking about you and trying to fig- ure out how to make things work," Kendall paused. "She loves you. She wanted to run from you, but she wanted your child to have his father. She wanted to come back and try and work through things with you."

"That may change once she realizes we lost the baby."

"It may, but not because she doesn't love you, but because she is having a hard time dealing with everything. Whatever happens, don't let her go. You two belong together. No matter what my dad says. Fight for her." Kendall squeezed his hand. "If it makes you feel any better, my mom is coming around. She thinks your good for McKenzie, too."

"Your dad's never going to like me."

"Maybe, maybe not, but he'll come around. You heard him the other day, he tolerates Braxton. He'll get to that point with you too."

"Oh, joy," he responds sarcastically.

"I love you," Kendall smiled.

"I love you, too."

"Hey," Braxton spoke up.

"Brotherly love," Kendall smirked.

"Okay, well as long as we keep at brotherly love, I'm going to head out. I think if I leave now, I can get to the stadium and be ready before game time."

"Okay, I love you," Kendall said as Braxton leaned over and kissed her," and not in that brotherly way," she smirked.

"I love you, too." He grinned back at her.

Marcus felt a twinge of jealousy watching them together. While he was happy for his friend, he wished he and McKenzie had that kind of relationship.

"Call me if you need anything or if there are any changes," Braxton commanded, "that goes for both of you."

"Okay," Kendall responded; Marcus nodded his head.

"I'll be back after the game to pick you up," he

told Kendall.

"Okay. Bring me and Marcus some dinner on your way back." She grinned.

"Yes, ma'am," he saluted as he headed out the door.

"I guess it's just us now," Kendall said as she laid her head on Marcus' shoulder.

"I wish McKenzie and I had what you and Braxton have," he told her.

"You will, in time," she replied. "Don't forget, we didn't always have this, we let way too many years slip away."

"I know and I'm not going to let time slip away from us."

"Good," Kendall stated as her parents walked back into the room.

"Where's Braxton?" Her mom asked.

"He had a game, since McKenzie pulled through everything okay, he decided to head on. He'll see her when he comes back to pick me up." Kendall responded.

"Marcus, are you staying the night again?" Mrs. Harper asked.

"Yes, ma'am," he politely responded.

"Okay, well since McKenzie is stable, we are going to head back home, go check on everything. We haven't been home since we landed. I just want to make sure someone was here with her at all times."

"I'm not leaving," Marcus responded.

"Please let me know if there are any changes, good or bad. Kendall can give you my number."

"Yes, ma'am. I will," Marcus responded as Mr. Harper took Mrs. Harper and lead her out of the room without saying a word.

"I'm going to go talk to my dad really quick. Meet you in McKenzie's room," Kendall said as she stood up and looked at Marcus.

"Okay," he responded as she headed out the door. He stood and grabbed Kendall's purse that was sitting on the chair, not wanting to leave it alone. He sent her a quick text letting her know he had it and then headed down the corridor to McKenzie's ICU room.

When he entered her room, he breathed a sigh of relief. She looked much better than she had been looking. The breathing tube had been removed as well as the EVD. She even had a little more color to her face. She did have a bandage wrapped around her head, but overall, she looked a lot better. He leaned over and kissed her forehead then pulled a chair up beside her and sat down. He took her hand in his and rubbed his hand up and down it before he kissed it.

"Hey, Baby," he started talking to her. "I don't know if you can hear me, but I'm going to talk to you anyway. I know I said some of this before, but I don't know if you heard me, so it bears repeating. Just so you know, once you open your eyes and come back to me, I'll repeat it again. I love you McKenzie Harper. I didn't think love was even in the stars for me, until I meet you. You're the one for me. You're the one I want to go to bed with each night and the one I want to wake up to each morning. I want to spend the rest of my life showing you how much you mean to me, but I can't do it until you wake up, so Baby, please wake up."

Marcus sat quiet for a moment and then started talking again, he wasn't sure what all he was talking about, but felt like if she heard his voice or someone she knew, she would wake up sooner. "You know, I was going to Vero Beach to see you as you were coming home to see me. I really wish you would have waited until I got there. Coming up on the accident scene and knowing that was you in that car knocked the breath out of me. I could barely breathe. I have never been so scared in my entire life, for you, for our baby. All I knew is I wanted to run down there and hold you in my arms. The police officer wouldn't let me. He told me I would only be in the way, so I let them do what they needed to do," he paused. "God, McKenzie, I have never loved anyone as much as I love you. You come back to me, you hear me. I can't do life without you." Marcus felt a hand on his shoulder at that last sentence. He looked up to see Kendall standing there with tears in her eyes.

"She's coming back to us Marcus, it may take some time, but she's coming back to us." Kendall squeezed his shoulder then pulled a chair up next to him. The two talked for a while.

Soon Braxton showed up with food for Marcus and Kendall. Eventually, he took Kendall home and Marcus was left there alone with McKenzie. He laid his head down on the bed beside her, without letting go of her hand, before long he had fallen asleep.

CHAPTER NINE

McKenzie slowly opened her eyes. It was dark outside, but the fluorescent lights in the room were bright. The brightness coming from them hurt her eyes, so she closed them and then slowly tried to open them again. She slowly took in her surroundings through slit eyes. Last thing she remembered was a deer jumping in front of her as she swerved to miss it, but where was she now?

She took in the white walls surrounding her, the beeping sound coming from the monitor and the IVs in her arm and realized she was in the hospital. She started to pull her arm up but couldn't. There was something heavy on it. She looked down at her hand and saw a head with dark blonde hair laying on it. Marcus. She grinned at first, then remembered why she was on the road in the first place. To get back to Marcus and talk about their future and the baby. *The baby.*

"Marcus wake up," the words were just a whisper coming from her voice. After the breathing tube and not talking for an extended period of time, her voice was weak. "Marcus," she tried again, rubbing his head. He slowly started to move, then jumped and looked up at her.

"McKenzie, Baby! Oh, my God, you're awake!" He said jumping up and kissing the top of her head and then her forehead.

"Marcus," she whispered his name again.

"Yes, love?" He stopped and looked her in the eye.

"The baby?" she questioned him.

He looked at her and did not say a word. The look in his eyes said it all. She burst into tears as Marcus leaned over and held her tightly. He just let her cry. Eventually after all her energy had been spent on crying, she fell back asleep. Marcus sat back down and pulled out his phone texting Kendall and her mother letting them both know that she had awoken but had gone back to sleep. He looked at his phone, it was two-thirty in the morning, he didn't expect to hear back from either of them tonight.

Marcus leaned over, kissed her forehead again and then sat back in the chair by McKenzie's bed. He put his hand on hers, laid his head back against the chair and then fell asleep.

After a couple of hours, Marcus started stirring in his chair. He woke to the sobs coming from next him. McKenzie had woken back up and was crying again.

He sat up and adjusted his seat, turning it so he was facing McKenzie and still able to hold her hand. "Kenz, we're going get through this."

"How?" she sniffled.

"Together."

"Marcus," she began, "I feel so guilty right now."

"It's not your fault, a deer jumped out in front of you."

"It's not just that. At first, I didn't want the child, not now, my career is just getting started. The thing is, while I was at Mom and Dad's I actually started getting excited about having a baby, being a Mom, but now I feel like I'm being punished because I didn't want it originally."

"Don't feel guilty about that. I was freaking out too. You cannot feel guilty about that. The initial shock was a natural reaction, we were not the first people to feel that way."

"I was going to be a mom. I wanted to be a mom, Marcus. I wanted to be our child's mom."

"You can still be a mom. Whenever you're ready, you let me know and I'll make it happen, whether it is the day we walk out of the hospital or three years down the road."

"That's just it, I don't know if I want to be a mom anymore. I don't know that I can risk the heartache of losing another child."

"Kenz, Baby, listen to me," Marcus put his finger to her chin and moved her face to where she was looking him in the eyes. "I think right now, you are scared and rightly so, but you do not need to make a decision today. I love you," she tensed at those words, "and I don't care if you want ten kids or none. I will support you whatever you decide."

"It's not fair to you. You need to find someone who will give you kids."

"Kenz, I want you, with or without kids. You are the only one for me."

"Marcus, don't," she sniffled.

"McKenzie, I'm not walking away from you and I'm not letting you go. Just know that."

"I need some pain meds," she said changing the subject.

"I'll call the nurse for you."

Later that morning her parents and Kendall showed up. The doctor had also come in to put a cast on her leg. Up until this point, they had not done it, due to surgery and being able to move her around easier. Since she was in a medical induced coma for most of the time, they knew she wouldn't be moving around enough to cause further damage.

Marcus had left for a few hours to go home, shower and change clothes leaving her alone with her parents.

"The doctor says you should be able to be moved to a regular room today and hopefully home in a few days." McKenzie's mother commented.

"Home, huh?" McKenzie responded.

"Yes. Your dad and I want you to come home with us. Let us take care of you. With the broken leg and watching for any signs of an infection from your EVD, it'll be better if your home with us where we can take care of you."

When her mom mentioned any infections from the EVD it reminded her of the partial shaving she now had due to the surgery. After Marcus had gotten the nurse to give her some pain medicine, they talked about everything that had happened from Marcus coming up on her accident up to the time she woke up. When he mentioned her head had been shaven for surgery she got upset. Since there was no mirror around, he took a picture on his phone and showed it to her. She began crying, even in the state she was in, she still held on to what little pride and vanity she had left. Marcus tried to reassure her, let her know that hair grows back, and they could look at wigs. She knew he was right but couldn't help but mourn for the loss of her hair, which turned into mourning the loss of her child again. He didn't try and tell it would all be alright or make light of it, he just let her cry.

He was good about letting her get out her frustrations without making light of things. He had also told her he loved her. Although she couldn't say it back, she knew in her heart of hearts that she loved him too, but right now just did not seem like the right time to explore that.

Marcus had been at her side every day, only leaving for short periods to go home and shower and grab her some food so she didn't have to eat the hospital food. She had gotten stronger and the doctor had finally given her permission to go home. Her parents and Marcus fought over who would take her home and take care of her. Ultimately, her parents won, well her father won. Her father was rude about the way in which he went about it. He didn't like Marcus and everyone in the hospital knew it. He told Marcus it was for the best, he needed to get back to baseball and he needed to let McKenzie get on with her life without him.

McKenzie didn't know if she agreed with that or not. However, she knew nothing could really come of their relationship. They lived in two different worlds. In the end, McKenzie told Marcus that he needed to move on and let her move on. He fought it, but eventually he left with Braxton and Kendall by his side.

CHAPTER TEN

Marcus sauntered into the locker room in a foul mood, just like every day since McKenzie had been released from the hospital and left with her parents. At first his teammates tried to console him, but eventually they realized it was doing no good. He would bite their heads off with some snarky misdirected comment, so they decided to back off and let him work through things on his own. Except for Braxton and Tex who had been best friends with him since the minor leagues.

"Marcus, pull your ass together, we have game to get through," Tex commented as Marcus grabbed his catcher's mitt out of his locker and threw it on the bench in front of him.

"Be there in a minute," he grunted. He grabbed his catcher's equipment and headed out onto the field.

Marcus was not concentrating out on the field, which threw Braxton off on his pitches. Eventually, Braxton had enough of it and called Marcus up to the mound.

"Look Marcus, you called me out on my shit when I was going through everything with Kendall. Now I'm calling you out on your shit. Right now, you're not communicating with me and it's making me look bad. You're going to end up getting us both benched. Pull your ass out of your butt and get your head in the game. We'll deal with McKenzie when the game is over, but right now you need to clear your head."

"Shit, you're right Braxton." Marcus said shaking his head. He knew he was not doing right by Braxton or the rest of his team. "It's not right to you or the team. I'll do my best to get her out of my head right now. Besides, she chose not to be with me. I need to move on. Do your change-up on this next batter. He always strikes out on those."

"That's my man. Let's do this," they fist bumped and Marcus headed back to home plate.

After a few more innings, the coach pulled some of his starters, including Marcus and Braxton and put in some of his rookies. After all, this was their time to shine and show him what they could do. Marcus sat on the bench and watched the others for a couple of innings and then decided to head into the locker room followed by Braxton and Tex.

"I'm heading home guys," Marcus stated after coming out of the shower and quickly throwing his clothes on.

"Braxton and I are heading over to your place too. Well order a pizza and watch the game. I think the Hawks are playing the Heat tonight." Tex stated as he pulled his jeans on.

"I'm good. You don't need to come over and baby-sit me. I'll see you guys tomorrow." He started to head out of the locker room.

"That wasn't a request, I think Tex said we were coming over." Braxton responded.

"Fine, whatever you want. Just don't expect me to entertain you," Marcus caved.

"You never do," Tex smirked as the three of them headed out of the locker room toward their cars.

As they exited the club house, there were several fans waiting at the exit, including some baseball groupies. Callie, who had gone out with Tex at one point and Summer who had gone out with Braxton once, were two of the groupies waiting.

"Hey girls" Tex drawled as they began to walk by.

"Hey Tex," Summer responded.

"Marcus," Callie cooed as she grabbed Marcus' hand. "What do you say, you and me? I can give you a night, you'll never forget."

"As well as some unknown disease," Tex whispered. Marcus looked at Tex and then walked over to Callie.

"What did you have in mind?" Marcus asked.

"First, I was thinking I would help you get out of these clothes," she whispered as she ran her fingers down his chest. "Then I'll wrap my lips around that nice thick cock I'm sure you have," she moved her hands down near his crotch.

"Um, Marcus," Tex said as he pulled him over, "Give us a second, sugar," he glanced at Callie.

"What the hell do you think you are doing, man?" Braxton asked.

"I think I'm getting some tonight. Might as well, it's not like McKenzie cares who I screw."

"Bullshit," Tex snapped.

"McKenzie still loves you," Braxton commented.

"Still loves me? She never loved me." Marcus grumbled.

"Let me repeat what I just said, Bullshit!" Tex responded.

"McKenzie has a lot to deal with right now, she lost her child," Braxton began.

"I lost my child too," Marcus interrupted.

"I know and that's why we've been putting up with your shit. Now shut up and let me finish what the hell I was saying," he griped at Marcus. "She has to rely on someone else to take care of her right now, she did not want to disrupt your life. If you were home taking care of her, you couldn't play baseball. To top it off, once she is healed and able to return to a normal life, as far as she knows, you are heading back to Atlanta and she'll be down here, not a good way to start a relationship."

"Did you tell her you were retiring after this year?" Tex asked.

"No," Marcus shook his head.

"Marcus," Braxton began, "Her father has been telling her it was a blessing in disguise that you lost the baby, that now she didn't have to deal with you anymore."

"What the fuck!" Marcus shouted. "How the hell do you put up with him?"

"Luckily, I don't have to see him often."

"I'm gone," Marcus said as he turned toward the parking lot.

"Where are you going?" Tex asked.

"To Vero Beach to get my woman back."

"She's not there," Braxton stopped him.

"Where is she?" Marcus looked at Braxton.

"She's in Atlanta, at my house. She got sick of her father telling her how bad you were for her and how losing your child was a good thing, so she went to stay with Kendall."

"How did she get there?"

"I went and picked her up the other day and

dropped her off at the airport."

"You didn't think to tell me this?" Marcus was irritated.

"She asked me not to say anything." Braxton said apologetically.

"So, you took her to the airport and let her go on an airplane in her condition? She had to be miserable in those seats."

"I made sure she was in first class, with a lot of room. Who do think I am?" Braxton asked.

"Thanks, man." Marcus threw his chin up.

"You need a ride to the airport?" Tex asked.

"Nah, I'll just leave my car in the parking deck. I'll need it to get to practice tomorrow." He turned again to leave when he heard his name being called.

"Marcus, are we going?" Callie asked from the line.

"No, sorry Callie. The rookies will be heading out soon, grab one of them. I'm sure they would be more than happy to go with you," he smirked then took off out into the parking lot.

CHAPTER ELEVEN

McKenzie sat on the couch feeding Josie a bottle as Kendall worked on making dinner and Jax sat on the floor playing a baseball game on his game station.

McKenzie glanced around, she loved Braxton and Kendall's house. It had a large open floor plan, making it where McKenzie and Kendall could easily converse while in separate rooms.

"I hate that can't I help with dinner." McKenzie commented.

"I'm good, don't need any help. Besides, your helping me by feeding Josie."

"I thought you were breast feeding."

"I was until I went down after your accident. She had to be bottled feed while I was gone. She does both breast and bottle now. I have to admit, it's kind of nice. At night before she goes to bed, I get that time with her while breast feeding, but during the day, it's nice to have a break, like right now," Kendall paused and looked at McKenzie. "Are you okay with her?"

"Yeah," McKenzie knew what she was asking. "At first, I was concern about being around Josie, but it's actually kind of nice, kind of cathartic."

"So, Dad actually said that it was a blessing that you lost your child?" Kendall asked.

"Yeah. Can you believe that?" She looked at her sister. "Who says that?"

"I don't know. I get that he doesn't like Marcus,

but that is just cruel."

"I agree," McKenzie paused. "Marcus is really not a bad guy. I mean hell, he stayed at the hospital the whole time with me, slept in that awful chair in the room. It didn't even recline."

"He's a good man," Kendall smiled at her.

"Why did he just let me go?" She looked at her sister with hurt in her eyes.

"You told him to." Kendall reminded her.

"True, but since when did he ever listen to me?" McKenzie could feel herself sinking back into the despair she had been in.

"Hey, I finally got you talking, don't shut down on me." Kendall commented. She could tell by the tone in McKenzie's voice that she was getting ready to shut back down. Since she had been there she had hardly eaten anything, she tried to stay upbeat for Kendall and the kids, but Kendall could see right through that. She would always disappear in the evening outside by the pool or the hot tub. Kendall tried at first to go out with her and talk to her, but quickly realized McKenzie needed that time to herself, so she usually let her retreat outside undisturbed.

"I don't know, Kendall. It's over. I head back to Orlando and a couple of weeks and he'll come back up here. We live different lives. I like my job, I'm not leaving Orlando and he can't leave Atlanta. It just wouldn't work out."

"If you really are meant to be together and if you really love each other, like I believe you do, you will find a way to make it work. I would suggest not letting ten years go by like Braxton and I did."

"I'm going to go change Josie's diaper," McKenzie

started to stand with her good leg, trying to avoid the subject.

"McKenzie, how are you going to carry her up the stairs on crutches? I'll go change her in a minute, let me get this in the oven."

"Yeah, okay," McKenzie sighed and settled back down onto the sofa.

"I got her," Jax responded as he headed over to McKenzie and carefully took his baby sister out of her arms then headed upstairs with her.

"Thanks, Jax," Kendall responded.

"He's a big help, isn't he?' McKenzie smiled.

"Yes, he is. He adores her. I'm telling you what, between Jax and Braxton, Josie is one spoiled little girl."

"Lucky little girl," McKenzie half-grinned thinking of what she lost and what she may never have.

"Give it time McKenzie," Kendall looked at her sister with a knowing look. "It will happen. You just need time to heal physically and emotionally."

"Am I crazy for walking away from Marcus?"

"Yes," Kendall didn't hesitate.

"Do you think he's worth giving up my career for?"

"I can't answer that for you, but I don't think you have to give up your career. I think you and Marcus can find a way to work things out."

"How long until dinner is ready?"

"About forty-five minutes to an hour," Kendall responded.

"I'm going to go outside for a little while." McKenzie just needed to go outside and think.

"Okay, I'll call you or send Jax for you when it's ready."

"Thanks," McKenzie responded as she stood up, grabbed her crutches and hobbled out the back door to the inground hot tub. It was a square hot tub which sat off to the side of the pool. She went to the left corner and sat down by it. She laid her left leg out straight on the concrete by the side of the hot tub. She then pulled up the leg of her black yoga pants, so they wouldn't get wet and stuck her other leg into the warm water.

March in Georgia was unpredictable. One day your wearing boots and jackets and the next shorts and flipflops. Today it was cool outside, but the warm water from the hot tub felt good. However, she had managed to hobble outside barefooted, in her yoga pants and a tank top, so she was a little cold. She shivered a little but shook it off as she looked off into the distance.

Out past Kendall's house was a pasture connected to a large farm. It was dark, so she really couldn't see much. However, she could see the outline of some horses thanks to the light from the moon. She saw a mare with its colt following close behind. She placed her hand on her stomach and sighed. As much as she wanted to cry, she didn't feel like she had any tears left. No matter what anyone else said she knew she was to blame for the loss of her child. She let her child down, she let herself down and she let Marcus down. How could he ever love her after she killed their child?

To top it off, it was her decision to leave town and run from Marcus. If she had just stayed and tried to work things out, then she would have never been on that road and none of this would have happened.

She would still be carrying their child. She didn't deserve to be happy. She didn't deserve Marcus and she sure as hell didn't deserve to be a mom. That being said, she still wanted to be a mom. She was scared though. She didn't think she could handle it if she lost another child. She had told Marcus at the hospital that she didn't want to be a mom any more, but being here with Kendall and holding Josie, she knew she really did want that, and she wanted it with Marcus. She also knew she couldn't have it. Whatever her and Marcus had. It was over, she had made sure when she walked away from him.

CHAPTER TWELVE

Marcus pulled up to Braxton's house in his white Mercedes-Benz GLS. He had grabbed an Uber at the airport and ran by his house to change clothes and grab his SUV which stayed parked in his garage while he was out of town. He knew McKenzie didn't have a car at the moment. He was hoping he could talk her into returning to Orlando with him and she could drive this car when she was able to get behind the wheel again. It was a lot safer than the Camaro she wrecked.

He got out of his SUV and slowly walked up to the door. He took in a deep breath and then knocked on the door. He was shocked when the door opened before he had time to step back.

"Uncle Marcus," Jax opened the door with a wide grin.

"Jax," Marcus said looking around for Kendall or McKenzie as he walked in giving a Jax a fist bump. "Shouldn't you ask who's at the door before you open it?"

"I knew it was you," he said pointing to a monitor, "and mom saw you pull up. She told me to get the door."

"Okay," Marcus responded looking at the elaborate alarm system Braxton had in place. He should have known after what Kendall went through with her ex kidnapping her that he would have something like that in place especially while he was out of town.

"Where is your mom?" Marcus asked.

"She's upstairs trying to get Josie to bed."

"Okay, well I'll try and keep it quiet then. What about Aunt McKenzie? Where is she?"

"She's out by the hot tub." Jax responded and then looked at up at him. "Uncle Marcus?"

"Yeah, Buddy." Marcus loved hearing him call him Uncle Marcus. When Kendall first came back into Braxton's life after ten years apart, she revealed a secret she had been keeping that entire time. Braxton had a nine-year-old son. When Marcus meet Braxton's son, Jax, they clicked right away. Marcus had told Jax to call him Uncle Marcus from the very beginning and it stuck. McKenzie ragged him about it forever, claiming he hadn't earned the title uncle, but in the end, he won out. Tex and Sawyer eventually became known as Uncle Tex and Uncle Sawyer as well.

"Can you make Aunt McKenzie feel better?" Jax asked. "She's sad. I hear her crying in her room every night."

"I'm going try and do the best I can. She's got some things she needs to work through."

"Yeah, Mom told me." He paused. "Uncle Marcus, I'm sorry about your baby."

"Thanks, buddy," Marcus ruffled his hair. "I'm going to go outside and see if I can't cheer your Aunt McKenzie up."

"Okay, I've got to go to bed." Jax turned to go up the stairs and then turned around to look at Marcus, "I'm glad you're here Uncle Marcus. Aunt McKenzie needs you."

"I'm glad I'm here, too. Good night, Jax." Marcus half- grinned at him and then turned around and headed out to the backyard.

Marcus quietly walked out onto the back deck and noticed McKenzie sitting off by the hot tub. Without saying a word, he took his shoes off, rolled up the legs of his jeans and then walked over to McKenzie. He sat down next to her, put his feet in the hot tub and his arm around her shoulders. She leaned into him and laid her head on his shoulder. He pulled her in and rubbed his hand up and down her arm. The two sat there for a good hour not talking, just holding each other.

"I lost our baby," McKenzie finally broke the silence.

"Kenz, Baby, we talked about this at the hospital. You cannot blame yourself for this. The deer ran out in front of you. You can't control that. I don't blame you and you shouldn't blame yourself." Marcus kissed her forehead.

"Marcus."

"Yeah, Baby."

"Remember when I said I don't want to have any more kids?"

"Yeah."

"Do you want kids?"

"McKenzie, look at me," he moved his fingers up to her face and rubbed them down her jawline before turning her to face him. He tried to think of how to say what he wanted to say without lying to her and without causing her to run again. "I'm not going to lie and say that the thought of having kids doesn't appeal to me because I would love to see kids running around the house one day, but Kenz, Baby you are what is important to me. I only want kids if you're their mother," he paused for a moment. "The thing is, we don't have to have kids. We always have Jax and Josie. We can also adopt or foster kids. Don't make a decision on us based on whether or not I want kids. I want you. The rest of it we can figure out."

"The thing is," she paused, "I think I still want kids." Marcus tried to hold his smile in. "After being here with Josie and holding her, I realize I want that too. I'm just scared. I can't lose another child."

"We'll first of all, we don't have to have kids right away. We can give ourselves time to adjust to being a couple before we add kids to the mix and time to mourn our child. As soon as you are ready, you let me know and we will get started making those babies."

"That's another thing." She looked at him. "I love you Marcus, but my job is in Orlando, your job is here in Atlanta, except six weeks out of the year. How are we supposed to be a couple? I mean how do we make that work? Especially if we add a kid or kids in the mix."

All of a sudden, she stopped and looked at him, confusion written all over her face. "How are you here now? Shouldn't you be in Orlando right now?"

Marcus smiled, squeezed her arm as he kissed her temple. "Yes, I am supposed to be in Orlando right now, but you are more important to me than any damn baseball game."

"It's not just a baseball game, it's your career."

"Well your more important to me than my career, but if it makes you feel better. I left after the last game this evening and our next game isn't until tomorrow evening." He sighed and continued, "back to us. I'm retiring after this year, so that leaves me free to move down to Orlando permanently."

McKenzie tensed up and then looked Marcus right in the eye. "Why?"

"Why, what?"

"Why are you retiring? I thought you, Braxton and Tex were going to go until you were well into your forties. Weren't you going to retire together? Is it because of me? I don't want you quitting your job because of me."

"Baby, listen to me. I'm not going to lie and say you don't play a big part in my decision, because you do. I love you more than I ever thought was possible. I want to be with you. That being said, most baseball players don't last more than five years. Braxton , Tex and I have all surpassed that. I have loved my job, but it is time for new blood to come in and take Atlanta even further than we ever did. Tex is going to keep going for a few more years, but Braxton is also retiring. He wants to be home for Kendall and the kids."

"Really? Kendall didn't say anything to me."

"I think they are waiting until it's official to say anything."

"What are you going to do if you retire? Won't you get bored? I don't want you resenting me because you left baseball."

"I could never resent you, Kenz," he smiled at her. "Braxton and I have been talking about starting up our own AAU baseball team. He would manage the Georgia chapter and I would manage the Florida chapter. I also talked to the coach and I would help coach the rookies each spring, so I would still be part of the Atlanta Eagles organization, so see Baby, I'm not stepping away from everything, I'm just making some changes." He paused for a minute. "Even if you say you don't want to be with me, I think it is time to retire. However, knowing that I'll be able to wake up with you next to me each morning, will make retirement so much better."

McKenzie looked at him with tears rolling down her eyes. She was speechless. She finally put her hands on his face and pulled him into her before crashing her mouth to his. "I love you Marcus Hunter."

"I love you too, Baby." He leaned in and returned the kiss before pulling back and looking her in the eye. "Go back to Orlando with me tomorrow. Please. I want you to stay with me. We will take my SUV and I'll leave it down there for you, so you'll have something to drive once the doctor gives you the all clear."

"Marcus, I don't want you SUV. I want another Camaro."

"I'm not going to lie and say I wouldn't rather you drive my SUV over the Camaro, especially after coming up on the car accident and seeing you trapped in the car. You don't have to keep it, but it gives you something to drive until you are ready to purchase a new car. Plus, I won't have to worry about how to get it down to Orlando once the season is over and I move down there. Not to mention, when you decide you're ready for us to have kids, we'll need it. My Porsche and your Camaro won't be conducive for a family."

"So, we drive back to Orlando tomorrow instead of flying?"

"Yeah, we'll just need to leave early, so I can get back for a six o'clock game." He smiled and looked at her. "Does that mean you're coming with me?"

"Yes, I'll come with you." She smirked."

"Hell yeah!" He grinned from ear to ear and leaned over and planted a big wet kiss on her lips. He then stood up and took her hand, helping her up. "Let's go to bed, we've got to get an early start tomorrow morning.

CHAPTER THIRTEEN

McKenzie woke up with Marcus' arms wrapped around her. The feel of his breathe against her neck sent shivers down her spine. She loved this feeling and knew every fiber of her being wanted to wake up like this each morning. It was crazy how good he made her feel.

They hadn't made love since the night she had gotten pregnant in December. Even last night, while Marcus kissed her lips and her neck tenderly a few times, he remained a gentleman. She wasn't sure if she was thankful or disappointed. Part of her wanted to just be with him and feel him, feel her skin against his skin. However, the other part of her, the scared part, was apprehensive about being with him again.

In the end, they packed up her clothing and other items, took individual showers and then crashed in the bed. She wore her loose pajama shorts and a tank top, and he wore his boxers. Even though he remained a gentleman and just held her tight, she could feel how much he wanted her between the thin layer of clothing separating them.

McKenzie started feeling movement and knew that Marcus was waking up. She moved to get up, but he pulled her back to him and began kissing the back of her neck.

"Good morning beautiful," he nuzzled into her neck.

"Good morning," she reached for his hand that was making its way under her shirt and toward her breast. She brought his hand up to her lips and kissed it then went to stand up. "I want to go say bye to Jax before he heads to school this morning since we will be gone before he gets home."

"I'll come with you. I want to say good-bye to him too," Marcus stood and walked over to where his jeans were laying across the chair. As he pulled them up and zipped them, he paused and looked at McKenzie, "You don't think Kendall will be upset I spent the night, do you?"

"Nah, we didn't do anything."

"And we weren't," he said looking at her. She gave him a why the hell not look, and he realized he better explain, or he would get himself in trouble. "Jax can hear through the wall."

"What?" She asked quizzically. "How do you know?"

"He said he could hear you. That you cried yourself to sleep each night. He was worried about you, wanted me to help make you feel better."

"Well crap," she said shaking her head. "I tried to hold it together in front of him. Poor kid." She sat down on her bed and looked up at Marcus, "He wanted you to make me feel better."

"Yeah," he half-grinned as he sat down beside her, wrapped his arm around her shoulders and pulled her into him.

She smiled at him, leaned over, kissed his cheek and then stood up, "Come on. Let's go say good-bye to him. It's going to take some time for me to work through this, but I'm going to put on a happy face for him and you can tell him, you made feel better."

"Anything you say, boss."

"Boss, I like the sound of that," she grinned.

"Don't get used to it," he smirked as she took his hand and they headed out of the room and toward the smell of coffee and bacon in the kitchen.

"Good morning, you two. Did you sleep well?" Kendall greeted them as she pulled down two coffee mugs and poured coffee into them.

"I did," McKenzie took the coffee from Kendall. "First good night's sleep I've had in a while."

Marcus grinned at McKenzie's confession. "Kendall, I hope it's okay that I stayed the night. I should've asked with Jax being old enough to know and all."

"Don't worry about it," she replied handing him a cup of coffee. "I don't think Jax even knows you spent the night. I just woke him up a few minutes ago to get ready for school. He'll probably just think you stopped back by this morning," she paused and looked at him, "well, except for maybe the bed head." She had to laugh at his dark blonde wavy hair that was sticking up all over the place. "Maybe hit the guest bath and straighten that out. There is an extra tooth-brush and toothpaste in there as well.

"Thanks," Marcus took a sip of his coffee and then headed toward the guest bathroom, but not before stopping to kiss Josie on the head. She was laying in her bouncer off to the side of the table.

McKenzie watched Marcus walk off into the bathroom and then turned to Kendall. "So, Marcus asked me to go back to Orlando with him."

"Are you going?"

"Yeah, I wanted to say good-bye to Jax before he heads to school. We'll head out right after that. He's got a six o'clock game tonight."

"Are you going back to your home or to his place?"

"His place for now." She paused and looked at Kendall. "I'm able to get around on my own pretty good. Other than the doctor hasn't released me to drive yet, but I'm not ready to be alone."

"Good," Kendall commented. "I don't think you need to be alone either and Marcus loves you. There is not a doubt in my mind about that."

"I know," McKenzie grinned.

"Know what?" Marcus asked as he headed back into the kitchen.

"That if we don't leave soon, you won't make it back for your game," McKenzie quickly tried to advert the conversation.

"Yeah, we do need to leave soon. Where's Jax?" Marcus asked just as Jax rounded the corner.

"You guys need to eat before you go," Kendall said placing two plates down on the table, before returning to the kitchen counter, grabbing two more plates and placing them on the table as well.

"You're leaving?" Jax asked looking at McKenzie and then Marcus.

"Yeah, we were waiting to say good-bye to you." McKenzie smiled. "Marcus has a game tonight he needs to get back for and I think it's time for me to head back home. I'll miss you," she leaned down and kissed his cheek.

Jax put on a brave face, "I'm going to miss you too, but I knew you would have to go back home soon." He gave McKenzie a hug and then looked at Marcus, "so if you have a game, you'll see my dad, right?"

"Right." Marcus grinned.

"Wait here, I have something for him," he instructed as he turned and ran toward his room.

"I won't move," Marcus said to the air, since Jax had already sprinted off.

"Here," Kendall said as she put two containers down on the kitchen bar. "I made some of Braxton's favorite cookies last night." Marcus opened one of the containers and looked in to find Cowboy cookies. He reached in to grab one as Kendall playfully slapped his hand away and closed the lid. "Those are for Braxton."

"Don't I at least get one for taking them to him?" Marcus asked giving Kendall a sad puppy dog face.

"Of course," Kendall laughed at him. I made a container for Braxton and one for you and McKenzie. Of course, I had to put some away for Jax," she winked.

"You made cookies for Braxton last night? I knew I smelled cookies baking, but how...?" McKenzie looked at her sister befuddled and then glanced at Marcus.

"I knew the moment Marcus showed up you would be leaving with him."

"You did?" McKenzie asked as Kendall gave a nod of her head with a smile across it.

"Come on, we need to eat. You need to get on the road and Jax needs to get to school," Kendall started to look around, "Where did he go?"

As if on cue, Jax came running back into the kitchen with two sheets of paper.

"Here," he hands the papers to Marcus.

"What ya got?" Marcus asked looking at the papers.

"This one is a test I took yesterday," he showed Marcus his paper which had a smiley face on it as well as grade written on it. "Dad helped me study for this the other night."

Marcus looked up at McKenzie puzzled, knowing Braxton was close to five hundred miles away, and then looked back at Jax.

"They Skyped," McKenzie chuckled.

"Oh," Marcus nodded in acknowledgement, then looked back at the paper.

"You made a 92? That's great!" McKenzie commented as she looked over Marcus' shoulder at the paper. "I know you were nervous about it."

"Yeah, Math is not my best subject, but Dad was able to help me understand it." Jax proudly announced.

McKenzie looked over at his test again and recalled the other night when Braxton was helping him over Skype. Even being hundreds of miles away, him and Kendall made it work. Braxton was still able to be present and a vital part of his kids' lives. Just thinking about that McKenzie finally grasped at the idea of how if you truly love someone you can make it work, just like Braxton and Kendall did.

"That's awesome, Jax." Marcus interrupted her thoughts. "What's the other paper?"

"I drew this for the Reflections program at school. Mom made a copy. I don't have the original. I won State, so my picture is going all the way to Nationals."

"Wow! That's great," Marcus responded as he looked down as the picture. "Is that your dad?" Marcus was astonished at what he was seeing. Jax had sketched a realistic pitcher who looked just like Braxton. He was in the process of throwing a pitch with one leg raised, his face glued toward the catcher and his hand pulling a ball from the glove on his other hand. Marcus continued to look at the picture and then focused on the catcher in the corner. The catcher, who was squatting at home plate with his glove open and ready to catch the ball, looked an awful lot like him. "Is that me?" He asked Jax.

"Yeah. I was going to put a batter in, but I couldn't figure out how to do it without covering you up."

"This is amazing Jax. Do you mind if I make a copy for myself?"

"No, that's fine," Jax grinned from ear to ear.

"So not only are you an amazing athlete like your dad, but your also an amazing artist like your aunt." Marcus remarked.

"Hey," Kendall responded. "I'm pretty good in the art department myself."

"Of course, you are," Marcus condescendingly smirked.

Kendall smacked him on the shoulder. "Let's eat before the food gets cold.

CHAPTER FOURTEEN

Marcus and McKenzie said their good-byes and were on their way back to Orlando. Marcus set up the back seat with two pillows, one for McKenzie's head and one for her foot, and a blanket. He was concerned about her foot being down for the long trip and with him trying to get back to the game, they were going to try and make as few stops as possible, which meant less time for her to stretch her foot.

Since Marcus had decided to drive back with McKenzie in order to leave the SUV with her, he needed to get his Porsche from the parking garage at the airport. He had talked to Braxton before leaving and asked him if he and Tex could go pick it up. Luckily, Braxton had a spare key to Marcus' house, so he would be able to get in and grab his spare car key.

"Are you sure we'll make it back in time for your game?"

McKenzie asked as they headed south on I-75.

"Yeah, we'll be there in time." Marcus laid his right hand on McKenzie's left thigh and smiled. "I'm so glad you decided to come back home with me."

McKenzie lifted Marcus' hand from her thigh and to her lips then kissed his fingertips.

"Are you okay with going to the game?" Marcus glanced her way, "I can drop you off at my place if you would rather go on home."

"I'll be fine," she smiled as she intertwined her

fingers with Marcus'.

"Good, because I want you there with me, but I should warn you," he paused, "Steffie will probably be there and she's very pregnant."

"I can't avoid pregnant women for the rest of my life," she half-grinned. Marcus took his thumb and rubbed it over her hand. McKenzie knew what she told Marcus was true. She had to be able to adjust being around pregnant woman and babies but was she really ready to be around Steffie without support. It would be different if Marcus was with her, but he would be on the field. After thinking it through, she decided she defiantly needed some kind of encouragement.

"Marcus," she looked over at him. "Is it too late to get another ticket? Can we get one for Piper? I want to believe I will be okay with Steffie, but it would be nice to have the added support."

"Of course, I'll call and have them add a ticket for her."

"Great," she smiled. "Let me call her first and make sure she can come. She's a big baseball fan, but I have to warn you, she's a huge Miami fan."

"Well I don't know if you need to be friends with her then," Marcus joked.

"Whatever," she smiled.

"Piper," Marcus began, "was she at Braxton and Kendall's wedding?"

"No, I don't think you've meet her yet. She was in Europe with her parents on vacation when they got married.

"Ooh, la, la, Paris," Marcus teased. "Her parents have money?"

"Yeah," McKenzie chortled. "Her dad is judge and her mother is a big fancy lawyer. They actually have a villa in Tuscany."

"Have you ever been to their villa?"

"Yeah, we went a couple of summers during college. It's nice. It looks more like a mansion than a villa. Have you even been to Italy?"

"No, believe it or not, I've never left the states."

"Big famous baseball player and you've never been outside of the states?"

"Nope."

"Guess we'll have to remedy that."

"Guess we will," he smirked. "Maybe on our honeymoon."

"Honeymoon?" McKenzie glanced at Marcus. "Slow down, there big wig. We haven't even defined this relationship yet. Think we are a few steps away from a honeymoon."

He glanced at her and smiled without saying anything. In his heart, he knew it was coming. It's what he wanted, and he was confident it was what she wanted too. "So, you've been to Italy," he decided it was time to change the subject for now, "is there anywhere you've not visited, that you would love to go to?"

"Greece and Ireland."

"Why Greece and Ireland?"

"I'm part Irish, so I've always wanted to go to Ireland, visit the castles and learn about my heritage."

"I can see that. Why Greece?"

"I don't know, I've always loved the Greek culture and food. In fact, there is a Greek community in the Clearwater area that Piper and I have gone to on occasion with our friend Mateo. It's quaint, the people speak Greek and the food is amazing."

"Mateo?"

"Yes, Mateo," she frowned her brows. "You're not jealous, are you?"

"No," he paused, "yes, maybe a little."

"Well, you know, I have heard some people refer to him as a Greek god," she smirked as she looked over at Marcus, his grip on the wheel tightening as his fingers turned white. "Relax, his boyfriend goes with us when we go."

"His boyfriend?" Marcus grinned.

"Yes, his boyfriend," she punched him in the arm. "I'm going to call Piper and see if she wants to meet me at the baseball field."

"Okay."

After a few minutes on the phone and an exchange of gossip, McKenzie hung up the phone with her friend.

"Piper's excited about going to the game, even though you don't play for Miami."

"I think you need to dump her. She's a bad influence on you. Miami, really?" Marcus shook his head. "Miami."

"She's excited about finally getting to meet you too."

"Yeah, well I'm excited about meeting my girl's best friend."

"Your girl?"

"Yes, and as far as defining our relationship as you mentioned earlier, I'm all yours exclusively and I want you to be all mine, exclusively."

"I have been," she paused, "since last year."

"Me too," he grinned.

"So, that there is no confusion. You are agreeing to officially be my girlfriend?"

"Yes, I am officially agreeing to be your girlfriend."

"Okay, good." He smiled looking straight ahead.

After a few moments of silence, McKenzie spoke up. "I think we should introduce Piper and Tex to each other."

"Piper and Tex?" Marcus chuckled.

"Yes, is there an echo in here?"

"I don't know, Tex can get his own girls."

"Yeah, I met Callie at the Christmas party."

"Hell, he just needed someone for the Christmas party and she was good for a one-nighter."

"Marcus!" She fiend shock. "Please tell me he didn't sleep with her."

"I don't know if he did or not," the green-eyed monster started showing in his face again. "Why are you worried about him?"

"He's been a good friend and I just want to see him happy. I think Piper could make him happy."

"You don't think he's happy now?"

"I don't know, maybe, but he could always be happier."

"McKenzie, I love you," Marcus began.

"I feel a but coming on."

"But, I don't think we need to meddle in Tex' love life. He's one of my best friends and Piper is one of yours. They are bound to come across each other. If it happens it happens, if not, then oh well. If we try and set them up and it doesn't work out, then we'll have to deal with the awkwardness between them and us.

"Huh," she sighed. "Party pooper."

"Can't say I've been called that before, but times are changing." He smirked.

A couple of hours later, McKenzie started moving around trying to adjust her leg. Marcus looked over and could tell she was uncomfortable. Without saying anything, because he knew she would argue, he pulled the car off at the next exit.

"What are you doing?" She asked.

"I need a restroom break," he smiled, "plus I need to top the gas off."

"Okay," she grinned. He could see relief in her face.

As he pulled up to the gas station, he looked over to McKenzie. "Why don't you get out and move around, then switch to the back. Your foot has been down too long."

"Yeah, it would probably do me some good," she said as she opened her door and stood there for a minute trying to gain her balance. Marcus pulled her crutches from the back and then walked over and handed them to her. He couldn't help but to lean over and lay a kiss on her lips in the process.

"Thanks," she returned the kiss.

After a short break and a full tank of gas, they were back on the road. McKenzie had crawled up into the back and propped her foot up on the pillow, then laid her head back and fell asleep.

CHAPTER FIFTEEN

Marcus pulled into the parking lot at the baseball field. He got out and walked around to the passenger door. McKenzie had moved back up to the front seat after there last stop. After helping McKenzie to step out, he grabbed her crutches and walked with her to her seat. After getting her settled in, he jumped the wall onto the field and headed toward the clubhouse to change. It didn't take long until he was back on the field dressed in his uniform.

Piper soon appeared, as well as Steffie, Jacob's pregnant wife, and some of the other wives and girlfriends. Piper recognized Steffie and Avery, one of the coaches' wives from events she had attended with Kendall. Some of the others she recognized from the Christmas party, but there were also some new girlfriends around.

"I can't believe you are wearing a Miami baseball shirt," McKenzie grumbled to her friend. "We aren't even playing Miami."

"Well, just because you have bad taste in men, doesn't mean I have to succumb to it. I mean Atlanta, really McKenzie?" Piper teased her.

"You better watch it, everyone around here is an Atlanta wife or girlfriend."

Piper looked around at the women who weren't paying much attention to their conversation and laughed. "Guess, they have bad taste like you."

"You better watch it, you'll be the next one married to an Atlanta baseball player."

"Not likely," she smirked. "However, I enjoy a good game." She nudged McKenzie's shoulder. "No, seriously. How are things going with you?" Piper turned serious.

"I'm fine," she half-grinned. "I'm doing better. I think spending some time with Kendall, Jax and even little Josie did me some good. I realize I do want kids one day. I'm sure when I do end up pregnant again, I'll be a nervous wreck, but Marcus will be too."

"Marcus, huh?" Piper grinned. "Does that mean you and him worked things out? I'm assuming you worked something out since you came home with him and we are sitting at an Atlanta baseball game getting ready to watch him play."

"Yeah, we worked things out. We are officially dating each other exclusively."

"Good. As much as I tease you about him playing for Atlanta over Miami, he's a good guy from what I can tell, and I think he's good for you."

"You haven't even meet him. How do you know?"

"Well, I know he was there in the hospital for you the whole time," Piper paused, "which, by the way, killed me being overseas and not being able to get home to you."

"I know, but you're here now."

"So is he," Piper smiled at McKenzie. "The man left his job here and went all the way to Atlanta to see you and bring you home. If that's not true love, I don't know what is. I would kill to have someone care that much about me."

"You'll find that one special person one day," McKenzie squeezed her friend's hand. She then looked out onto the field and saw Tex tossing the ball to Braxton. "You never know, it may be sooner than think."

"Yeah, wishful thinking, right?"

"Hey, listen," McKenzie began, "I've got to run this by Marcus first, because I'm not sure of his schedule, but maybe one day this weekend you and some of his friends can come over for a cookout."

"Sure, just make sure you invite some of his single friends," Piper winked, "or don't because they play for Atlanta and that just won't work."

"You are going to end up marrying an Atlanta baseball player, just watch and see," McKenzie laughed at her.

"Don't hold your breath," she chuckled as she glanced toward the field. "Game is starting."

Braxton winds up and throws his first pitch. The batter swings and strikes out as the ball flies straight into Marcus' glove.

"So which player are you wanting to set me up with?" Piper asked.

"I don't know what you are talking about." McKenzie fiends shocked.

"Oh, okay," Piper sarcastically remarked. "Which one is Tex?"

"The short stop. Why?"

"Well, because other than Marcus, you talk an awful lot about him. If Marcus wasn't in the picture, I would almost think you have a thing for him."

"Tex has become one of my best friends. He is easy to talk to and he calls bullshit on Marcus when he acts like an ass."

"He's the one you are wanting to set me up with, right?"

"I didn't say that," McKenzie glanced the other way.

"You didn't have to say that," she commented as she watched the batter hit the ball down the line between 2nd and 3rd base. Tex leaned in and swooped the ball up, throwing it toward 1st base for an easy out. "He's good."

"Yeah, he is." McKenzie agreed, "he's good-looking too."

"Yeah, if you're in to tall muscular men," Piper breathlessly responded.

"You might want to wipe that drool off your mouth," McKenzie laughed.

McKenzie and Piper watched the rest of the game and chatted with the wives and girlfriends that sat around them. Steffie and McKenzie who were close to Braxton and Kendall were especially concerned for her well-being.

As the game came to an end and Atlanta walked away with a win, Piper and McKenzie gathered their things and headed out to the line near the clubhouse entrance where the fans waited for the players to exit. McKenzie and Piper stood off to the side watching all the hoopla.

"Baseball groupies?" Piper asked looking at a couple of women dressed in tight Daisy Duke shorts and tighter Atlanta shirts.

"Yeah, just wait. They'll be all over the guys when they come out." McKenzie said in disgust. "I recognize one of them over there." She nodded toward Callie.

"Do you think any of the baseball players have actually ended up married to one?"

"I don't know, maybe somewhere, but not any of these guys. There good for a one-night stand, but that's about it. The sad thing is, some of them will sleep with every one of them if they could. Just watch when the guys start to come out."

As if on cue, Braxton, Marcus and Tex came strolling out of the clubhouse.

"Marcus," Callie crooned, "how about that date you promised?"

"I didn't promise anything, Callie?" Marcus replied and then looked over toward McKenzie. "I've got to go, my girlfriend is waiting for me."

"Your girlfriend?"

"Yeah,' he nodded toward McKenzie and then headed her way.

"Braxton?" Callie turned her claws toward him.

"I'm married Callie."

"Yeah, but she's not here."

"I'm not even going to dignify that," Braxton turned and walked off.

"Callie, show some class." Tex commented as he started to walk by her.

"That's not what you were saying when I was under you a few months ago," she boasted as she grabbed a hold of his arm.

"Yeah, well that was a mistake I won't make again." He pulled his arm away and headed over toward Marcus and Braxton.

"You slept with her!" McKenzie shouted out as Tex approached them.

"I blame it on the whiskey," he responded.

"Did you have a lot of whiskey?" McKenzie question.

"Nope, I'm just blaming it on the whiskey," he smirked.

"So, you just sleep with any bimbo that throws herself at you?" Piper asked.

"I'm sorry, who are you darlin'?" Tex inquired.

"Tex, this is my friend Piper," McKenzie jumped in.

"Well Piper, it's nice to meet you. Any friend of McKenzie's is a friend of mine, but I'm sure my sex life is none of your business. At least until I get to know you better darlin'" he winked at her.

"Ugh," Piper rolled her eyes.

"I'm taking McKenzie home. We left at eight this morning and haven't been home yet." Marcus addressed his friends.

"I'm heading out, too. I'm going to go home and call my family." Braxton commented.

"We'll walk with you. We have some things in the car for you from your wife and son." Marcus responded as he looked over at McKenzie, "ready, Babe?"

"Shouldn't someone walk Piper to her car?" McKenzie asked.

"I'm good, I don't need anyone to walk me."

"I'll walk you, Darlin'." Tex smirked.

"Oh joy,' Piper sarcastically responded as her and Tex headed toward her car.

Marcus turned and looked at McKenzie as they walked toward the car with Braxton. "See that's why I didn't want to try and set Piper and Tex up. They are going to kill each other before they get to her car."

"I don't know," Braxton interrupted. "I think they'll end up in the bed together. They remind me of you two in the beginning, all the bickering back and forth."

"We didn't bicker," Marcus responded.

"Bullshit," Braxton coughed.

"Yeah, we did," McKenzie laughed, "we still do."

As they got to the car, Marcus opened the passenger door and got McKenzie settled in and her crutches put up before gathering the papers Jaxson had sent down as well as the cookies Kendall sent and handed them to Braxton.

Braxton looked at the Math paper Jaxson had sent, and you could the pride in his face. He was also impressed with the sketch Jaxson had drawn and couldn't wait to get home to Skype with him and let him know how proud he was of him. Braxton was also excited about the container of Cowboy cookies Kendall had sent. He opened the container and began eating the cookies as he strolled off toward his car.

CHAPTER SIXTEEN

After a long day of traveling and then a ballgame, Marcus pulled his Mercedes Benz SUV into his driveway next to his Porsche which had been retrieved from the airport. He slowly pulled himself out of the car and then headed over to help McKenzie out. He grabbed the bags from the car and the two of them headed into his town home located right across the street from Braxton, Tex and Xander's homes.

Several of the baseball players had town homes in the gated community where he lived. It was easier to purchase the town homes then stay in a hotel during the six weeks they were down for spring training.

Marcus, like several of his teammates would let family and friends borrow his town home when he wasn't using it. However, lending his town home out was probably coming to an end soon. He was going to try and talk McKenzie into moving into it since his town home was bigger than her apartment. At least until they started having kids, then he would need to sell it and buy a house.

"Why don't you go take a shower while I get everything out of the car?" Marcus asked, then looked at her cast. "Can you take a shower in the cast?"

"Yeah, it's waterproof, or water resistant. I can't stay submerged in it, but if it gets wet it won't hurt it."

"Okay, let me get you set up," He motioned her toward her his room. He went into the bathroom and started the shower. He placed a towel and washcloth by the sink for her. Then headed back into his room where she was sitting on the edge of his bed. "The shower is going, I laid a towel and washcloth by the sink. I don't have any smell good shampoo and soap, but you can use what I have," he paused and looked at her. "It'll be kind of sexy having you smell like me."

"Marcus," McKenzie rolled her eyes as she walked by him and into the bathroom.

Marcus went to his drawer and pulled out one of his t-shirts and quietly opened the bathroom door. McKenzie was just pulling off her shirt and turned to look at him.

"Don't mind me," his gaze looked her over, "I'm just dropping off a shirt for you," he laid the shirt next to the towel, smiled and reluctantly walked back out of the bathroom.

After emptying the car, he took McKenzie's bags back to his room and laid them against the wall. He needed to clean out some drawers, so she could unpack her things. He would do that tomorrow morning. Tonight, they needed to shower, eat and head to bed.

Marcus headed back into the kitchen and threw together a couple of BLT sandwiches, carrots, pita chips and hummus. He grabbed a beer for himself and a water bottle for McKenzie.

Just as he was laying the plates of food at the table, McKenzie came out in his t-shirt. He stopped in his tracks as his eyes roamed up and down her body, taking in her sculpted legs, which looked like the legs of a dancer. Her damp, long, wavy, dark hair and the way the shirt hung on her body stirred him from inside. He could feel his pants getting tighter and knew he needed to look away.

"You know, I have never seen anything sexier than you in my t-shirt." He grinned as he managed to set the plates down.

"I bet you say that to all the girls," she commented as she hobbled over to a chair and sat down.

"You're the only one that has been in my t-shirt."

"Your telling me that not one girl, put your shirt on after one of your one-night stands?"

"No, it's too intimate. I usually pulled myself together pretty quickly and headed out. Didn't stay long enough for them to be able to grab it," he looked away somewhat ashamed.

"Wearing your shirt was more intimate than having sex with them?"

"Yeah, sex was just sex. I was just fucking them," he paused. "Shit, that sounds harsh."

"Yeah, it does. So, what we did was just fucking?"

"Hell, no! What you and I did, and will hopefully do a lot more of, is make love," he paused again and looked at her, "You know you are the only woman I have been with since we meet last year. You're the only one I've wanted to be with."

"What about Callie?" McKenzie looked at him. "What did she mean when she said you promised her a date."

"I didn't promise her a date," he ran his hand through his hair. "When you left and went to your parents' house I tried so hard to get in touch with you. You ran from me and you wouldn't take my calls, for a moment, and just a moment, I almost gave up on you, on us. She offered a night I wouldn't forget," Marcus could see McKenzie tensing up as he told her what happened, but he did not want any lies between them. "I agreed, but then before anything could happen, I changed my mind. That's when Braxton told me you had gone to his house, so I left her standing there and went after you. Well, I did tell her to go for a rookie," he smirked.

"Oh," McKenzie wasn't quite sure what to say. "Thank you for being honest with me."

"I won't lie to you about anything McKenzie. You may not like what I have to say, but I will always be upfront and honest with you." He picked up his sandwich and took a bite into it while she let what he said sink in.

They finished eating their dinner in silence. Both were exhausted and ready for bed. Once they finished eating, Marcus cleared the table. McKenzie tried to hobble around and help, but Marcus wouldn't hear of it. Since Marcus refused to let McKenzie help any, she conceded and headed back to his bedroom to retire.

He soon joined her in the room, she was already in the bed and under the covers. He had taken a shower at the clubhouse before heading home, so he retreated to the bathroom to brush his teeth and face then headed back into the room. He stripped down to his boxers and crawled into the bed behind McKenzie. He wrapped his arms around her, her back to his front and spooned her. The two of them quickly drifted off to sleep.

CHAPTER SEVENTEEN

McKenzie woke up the next morning with one arm across her waist and a hairy leg across her leg. She couldn't move from the bed if she wanted to. The thing was, she really didn't want to. She liked waking up to Marcus wrapped around her. However, she really did need to use the bathroom, so she slowly tried to move his arm and leg and then slid out of the bed.

As she headed into the bathroom, she noticed her make-up bag on the sink. She opened it up and pulled out her toothbrush, toothpaste and mouthwash. She took a washcloth and washed her face and then decided she would head into the kitchen and make some coffee.

McKenzie headed out of the bathroom and back into the bedroom. She glanced over to the bed and saw Marcus sitting up with his back against the headboard smiling at her.

"Good morning, Love," he grinned.

"Morning," she smiled back. "I was going to go make some coffee."

"That can wait," with his finger, he motioned for her to come to him.

"She hobbled over to the bed and crawled into it. He pulled her closer to him until her face was inches from his face. He leaned down and engulfed her mouth with his. She returned the kiss with passion. She opened her lips enough to allow his tongue to thrust into her mouth and explore each part of it. In return she thrust her tongue in between his lips until the tongues were inter-twined and playing a friendly game of tongue war with each other. She finally pulled away to catch her breath. When she did he pulled her down and positioned himself over her.

She wanted him more than she wanted her next breath, but she was nervous. This would be their first time to-gether since she had gotten pregnant and lost their baby. He seemed to sense it. How was it, he could read her so well?

"It's okay, Baby," he balanced his body on the side and then ran one hand down her arm. "Are you on birth control pills?"

"No," I was pregnant and then after I lost the baby I just didn't think I would be with anyone else after you. At least for a while. I didn't expect us to get back together. "Do you have condoms?"

He reached over her and opened up his drawer. He pulled out a brand new box of condoms and proceeded to unwrap the box before pulling out a foiled package. "I promised myself, I would be prepared next time we were together. Not that I didn't have any around last time, I just think we wanted to be with each other so bad, we didn't think about it."

"Well, put that bad boy on and make me feel like a woman," she smirked.

"You sure," he looked at her, "I don't want to push you."

"You're not pushing me, I want to be with you. I need to feel you inside me."

"Well, my plight in life is to make sure all your wants and needs are meet." He smiled as toyed with his shirt which she was wearing and then helped her sit up while he pulled it off of her, revealing her naked body. He revered in her body as he gazed up and down her body while licking his lips.

"I slept next to you all night with nothing under the t-shirt," he stuttered.

"Yep," she grinned.

"If I had only known," he growled as his fingers moved down to her breast where they stopped to play with her nipples. He slowly replaced his fingers with his teeth, nipping at them, causing her to moan. His fingers continued to make their way down her tight stomach until they reached her heat. He moved his fingers slowly in and out, reaching in and hitting her G-spot. Soon he was thrusting his fingers in and out quickly. He mouth released her nipples as he moved down to position himself between her legs and began to taste her with his tongue, flicking at her clit as he tasted the sweetness nixed with salty of her. Replacing his tongue with his fingers, he began thrusting again until she climaxed. With the satisfaction of making her come, he pulled himself back up and ripped open the foil package. He quickly rolled it on and then gently moved back and forth until the mushroom head slowly entered into her. He gently pushed in until he could go no further and then pulled back out. She arched her back and moaned.

"Faster, please," she pleaded. That was all it took, he began thrusting in and out as he penetrated her. She moaned and called out his name. All at once she hit another climax. The contraction on his cock as she climaxed sent him over the edge and he too climaxed releasing his seed into the condom.

Marcus collapsed on McKenzie and then rolled off her. He lay beside her, both of them sated. After a couple of minutes, he finally stood up and then went to the bathroom relieving himself of the condom. After washing his hands, he returned to bed and pulled her into him.

"I don't think I will ever get tired of this," he grinned.

"You better not," she rolled over and kissed him and then sat up and reached for the t-shirt.   "I'm going to go make breakfast."

"Let me," Marcus responded as he reached for his boxers. "You need to stay off the foot."

"I'm not an invalid," she replied, "besides it should be coming off next week. I go see the doctor and if all is well, he'll move me to a walking cast."

"Okay, let's make breakfast together," Marcus decided to compromise.

Marcus and McKenzie made their way into the kitchen. They worked around each other like they have been doing it forever. After a hardy breakfast of Eggs, bacon and toast, they cleaned up and made their way back into the bedroom.

Marcus cleared out a few drawers and some space in the closet to make room for McKenzie. He helped her unpack her things and get them situated. After all McKenzie's things had found a home, they took a shower together. While Marcus wanted to throw her against the tile walls of his shower and make mad passionate love to her, he was scared if they slipped she could hurt herself, so they were both content with washing each other until after the shower when Marcus picked her up and threw her on the bed, where he made love to her two more times before having to get up and get ready for practice and a game.

CHAPTER EIGHTEEN

It had been a week and Marcus and McKenzie had settled into a nice routine. Through everything that had happened over the last several weeks, between the pregnancy, McKenzie's running off to her parents, the accident, running off to her parents again and then Kendall's spring training seem to have flown by. There was only a week left and then Marcus and McKenzie would have to deal with what came next.

Marcus would have to travel with his team, that was a given. McKenzie would need to get back to work. Thank goodness she was due to get her cast removed this week. That would make it easier for her to get around without Marcus there to cater to her. Although she really didn't need to be catered to, but Marcus liked taking care of her. He knew she had caved and let him think he was helping her. He knew when he was gone during the day, she maneuvered around just find without him. She often had dinner ready for him when he got home. In addition, the other day, when he got into his SUV, he could tell she had been in it. He had to readjust the seat and mirrors.

Marcus kissed McKenzie and headed out the door to his game. Avery, one of the wives, was going to stop by and pick her up before the game today and then she would ride back home with Marcus. She had gone to some of the games this past week but not all of them. She had stayed home some to work on a project she needed to have completed by the end of the week.

Marcus walked into the clubhouse and changed into his practice uniform before heading out onto the field. He had talked to the head coach the other day and told him about his plans to retire after this season was over. The coach told him he was not surprised, he figured with Braxton retiring, Marcus was not far behind. Him and Braxton were almost a package deal. As such, the coach had him and Braxton working with the rookies. The coach wanted another duo that worked together as well as Braxton and Marcus and put them in charge of finding the duo. Marcus knew what he and Braxton had was something special. They could probably find a pitcher and catcher who worked well together, but the dynamics they had would not be the same as him and Braxton.

"So, we have seen a couple of these rookies together. Who are you thinking shows the most potential here?" Marcus asked Braxton.

"I don't know. I think Camden is the best pitcher we have, next to me of course," Braxton smirked.

"Of course," Marcus chuckled.

"He has the fastball and split finger fastball down. He's also really good with the slider and curveball. In all sincerity, I've yet to see a pitch he doesn't exceed in. Put a few years of experience under his belt and he's going to break some records."

"Luca has been on top of things. He can tell you exactly which pitches the batter struggles with. He studies before the games. I've quizzed him, and he's been on top of it. On top of that, he moves fast and can anticipate the pitch heading his way."

"Camden normally pitches to Trenton and

Mitchell pitches to Luca. Let's try and put Camden and Luca together and see what kind of chemistry they have together. We'll put Mitchell and Trenton together and see how they do together as well."

"Call me crazy, but I kind of like working the field from this angle as much as being the player." Braxton commented.

"I do too, retirement may not be so bad. Coach told us we had training positions during spring training each year. It'll be nice to still be a part of the organization."

"Yeah, it will." Braxton patted Marcus on the back as he headed toward the bullpen.

Before long, it was game time. The guys had gone back into the clubhouse to change into their game uniforms. Marcus looked up to the stands and saw McKenzie up there and smiled. He loved her being in the stands and more importantly the fact that she was there for him made his heart flip. He never thought he would ever feel this way about someone. He had been burned by groupies just wanting to be with him because of what he did for a living not because of who he was as a person.

Braxton and Marcus were in the starting line-up but only played the first two innings. It was decided to let Camden and Luca play the next few innings and then Trenton and Mitchell to see how they performed together during the game. As suspected, Camden and Luca were in sync with each other. An observer would have never guessed that this was their first time playing together.

"Yes, I think we just found our replacements." Marcus fist bumped Braxton.

As the game to an end, with a victory for Atlanta, the guys headed back to the clubhouse.

"Hunter," the head coach called.

"Yes, Coach"

"Get showered and dressed and come see me in my office."

"Yes, sir."

"Oh, and Marcus," Coach Anderson paused, "you might want to see if one of the guys can take McKenzie home, if she was planning on riding with you."

"I will," he said as he turned around and eyed Braxton with a confused look on his face.

"I'll take McKenzie home," Braxton said wearing the same confused look on his face as Marcus. "Call me and let me know what's up."

"Sure," Marcus said as he sauntered toward his locker and grabbed his toiletries for a shower. He quickly showered and dressed anxious to find out what was going on.

"Coach?" Marcus knocked on the door.

"Come in Marcus, have a seat," he motioned to a chair across from his desk. "I'm not going to pussy-foot around this, I'm just going to come right out with it," the coach spat out. "Do you know a Holly Wright?"

"I can't say I do," Marcus responded. "Why?"

"She claims you are the father to her child."

"What?"

"Look, you know as well as I do, all kind of cra-zies come out of the woodwork trying to trap a base-ball player. Since Kendall came into the picture with Jaxson the numbers of call have increased. We scan the calls and do the best we can in not letting them get through to you, but this one seems legit." Coach Anderson commented as he slid a picture across the table to Marcus.

"Who's that?" Marcus asked looking at a picture of a blonde headed little girl. She looked to be about four years old.

"Supposedly your daughter, Emma."

"Shit!" Marcus ran his hands through his hair, "it's not possible, other than McKenzie I have always used a condom." He paused, "Shit! Shit! Shit!" After running his hands over his face over and over again, he finally looked back up at his coach. "I want a blood test."

"We told her that and she has agreed to it." The coach went into further details into the woman, her claims and where everything allegedly happened.

"Fuck! McKenzie is not going to handle this well. Especially after the accident. She's just starting to come around. I should have known things were going to well for us."

"I'm sorry," the coach sympathized. "Head by the clinic, they are expecting you. They'll draw your blood, once the results from the blood test comes in, I'll give you a call."

"Okay," Marcus solemnly responded as he stood up and headed out of the office.

CHAPTER NINETEEN

After running by the clinic and getting his blood drawn, Marcus drove around for a while before calling Braxton.

"Hey," the Braxton's voiced came from the other end of the phone. "So, what did coach want?"

"I'm so screwed."

"Why? What is going on?"

"Did you get McKenzie home?"

"Yeah, I even watched her go in before I headed over to my place."

"What did you tell her?"

"Coach had called you back and you didn't how long it would be." Braxton paused, "Are you going to tell me what is going on or not? I know you're not being traded since you are retiring at the end of the season, so what the fuck is up?"

"Some girl named Holly called in and claimed I'm the father to her four-year-old daughter."

"Well, shit!"

"My sentiments exactly."

"Did you demand a blood test?"

"Yeah. Coach said he had already mentioned it and she agreed to it. I went to the clinic and had my blood drawn, but if she is agreeing to a blood test that easy..." Marcus didn't finish his sentence.

"I was thinking the same thing."

"Fuck, Braxton. What am I going to do, McKenzie

is going to go ape-shit when I tell her. I don't know if she'll be able to handle it. I may lose her because of this," he paused "and things were just starting to work with us."

"Well, first of all, you need to tell her as soon as you get home. If she hears it from anyone else she won't forgive you. I'm not going to lie, it's probably going to be rough at first because of all she's been through, but whatever you do, don't give up on her," Braxton paused, "she may need some time to adjust though."

"Shit! I can't lose her."

"Well tell her right away."

"Would it be bad if I seduce her first, before telling her? I mean, it may be my last time to have sex with the woman I love."

"Love? That's the first time I've heard say love in regards to McKenzie."

"I've told her it, plenty of times."

"I knew you loved her, I just hadn't heard you say it."

"Don't say anything to Kendall, please."

"About the love or the child?"

"The child, you dick."

"I won't, but you need to say something to McKenzie as soon as you get home."

"I just pulled in the driveway. If you hear screaming..." he trailed off.

"Good luck man. Call me after things calm down and let me know how it went."

"Yeah." Marcus replied as he hung up the phone. He put his car in park and then laid his head down on the steering wheel. This was not going to go well. He just knew it.

Marcus pulled himself together and headed inside. As he walked in, he looked over and saw McKenzie in the kitchen. She had obviously taken a shower and changed after getting home from the game. She looked beautiful standing there in her black running shorts and pink tank top with the Atlanta symbol on it. As if sensing his eyes on her, she slowly turned around and smiled.

"Dinner is almost ready."

"Good, I'm starved." He forced a smile.

"What did the coach want? You were there for a while."

"Let's eat first, then I'll tell you." He wanted to get in one final meal with her.

"That bad?"

"Well talk after dinner. Baby," he walked over, placed his hand on the small of her back, pulled her in and kissed her forehead. He was going to savor ever second with her.

After a somewhat quiet dinner, Marcus and McKenzie cleaned up the dishes and then headed over to the living room. Marcus wrapped her hand in his as he led her to the sofa. She sat down and then he sat beside her with his body turned facing her.

"So, you know before you I was sexually active," Marcus began.

"Who's pregnant?" McKenzie pulled her hand away from his.

"Ever since you came into my life, I've not been with anyone but you," he paused giving McKenzie a moment to talk. When she didn't say anything, he continued. "You are also the only woman I've not used a condom with." She continued to look at him without saying anything, so he kept going. "There is a woman named Holly claiming that I am the father to her child."

"Do you remember a Holly?" McKenzie finally spoke in an eerily calm voice.

"I don't," he paused, "I'm ashamed to say this, but that doesn't mean anything. I don't remember a lot of the groupies."

"Where did this, um, conception happen?"

"San Diego."

"Did you ask for a blood test?"

"Yes."

"And she consented?"

"Yeah."

"Hmm."

"McKenzie, I love you and I don't want to lose you. Whatever happens, you have to know you are still my priority."

"Marcus, I'm tired. I'm heading to bed." McKenzie stood up and started to the bedroom, but before she disappeared into the hallway she turned around and looked at Marcus. "If you have a child, that should be your first priority."

Marcus watched her walk off before he bowed his head and buried it in his head. After a few minutes he heard his phone ping. He pulled it out of his pocket and looked. He had a message from Braxton

Braxton: ???

Marcus: Ever hear of the calm before the storm?

> *Braxton: Yeah.*
>
> *Marcus: She was eerily calm when I told her.*
>
> *Braxton: That's not good.*
> *Marcus: That's what I'm thinking. She's already retired to the bedroom. She didn't leave.* That's good, right?
>
> *Braxton: Hopefully.*

Marcus pocketed his phone and headed into his room. He slowly opened the door, when he saw McKenzie already in the bed, he sauntered into the room. While she lay there with her eyes closed, he could tell she was not asleep. He knew the difference in her breathing from when she was and wasn't asleep. While nothing was spoken, he could feel the tension. For right now, he was just thankful she was still there.

He went to the bathroom and got ready for bed. After brushing his teeth and discarding his clothes, minus his boxers he headed back into the room. He crawled into the bed, as he pulled the covers up to get in, he noticed she was in sweatpants and a t-shirt. She never wore sweatpants and t-shirt to bed. Hell, she never wore sweatpants and a t-shirt around the house. Maybe, just his t-shirt, with nothing underneath. She was definitely upset, but again at least she was still there, in his bed, and she was wearing his t-shirt.

McKenzie was facing the wall, with her back to him. He edged up close to her, his front to her back, wrapped his arm around her waist and spooned her.

She didn't move away or toward him. Normally, she would wiggle backwards until they were snugged tightly together. She just laid there like a log. He almost wished she would just yell at him. The cold shoulder was almost worse. How could things go from being so great to being so fucked up so quickly? All he knew was that he loved McKenzie and they were going to make this work, some way, somehow.

CHAPTER TWENTY

McKenzie woke up the next morning, Marcus had one arm and one leg wrapped around her like he was scared she would escape. She slowly moved his arm off her and carefully slide out from under his leg. She quietly made her way into the bathroom to wash up and brush her teeth. She looked at the dark circles under her eyes caused from the lack of sleep.

She heard Marcus come into the room and closed her eyes. She felt him crawl in beside him and refused to give in. Logically she knew that this problem was caused because of something he did before they meet, but it did not make it hurt any less. On top of that, if he did have a child, that would change the dynamics of their relationship.

While his comment about her being his first priority should have comforted her, it didn't. How dare he put anyone before his child, if the child was indeed his. Would she really want to be involved with someone who could disregard his child so easily?

As much as she wanted to grab her stuff and walk out, she decided she would make breakfast and send him off to practice. Then she would decide what she needed to do. Throwing on a pair of blue jeans and a form fitting powder blue t-shirt she scooted out of the room and toward the kitchen.

Marcus sauntered into the kitchen. His eyes lit up when he saw her. Walking over to the counter where she was whisking away at the eggs, maybe a little too harshly, he leaned over and kissed her on the head.

"Good morning," he greeted her.

"Morning," she muttered.

"McKenzie," Marcus began.

"Eat, you've got to get to practice," McKenzie sat the plate in front of him, interrupting him, not wanting to hear what he had to say.

The two sat in silence eating. McKenzie could tell Marcus wanted to say something but wasn't quite sure what to say. She was glad because she didn't want to talk about it right now. She knew she loved Marcus, but if this child turned out to be his, could she deal with it. How would they handle custody, the child lived in San Diego? Would Marcus move there? Would he expect her to move there? Would he try to see his child or just send money? The comment he made last night about her being his first priority made her wonder. She had a lot to think about and she needed to do it away from Marcus. She was glad he was getting ready to head to work.

"I've got to go, Baby, " Marcus stood and took his plate to the sink and then wondered over to her, leaned down and kissed her on the lips. "We'll talk when I get home?"

"Yeah," she nodded as she watched Marcus walk out the door.

As soon as he was gone, she walked back into the kitchen and began cleaning the dishes. She straightened up the living room and then went back into the bedroom. As she was straightening up the bedroom, she saw the picture Marcus had received of the child who was possibly his child, a little girl, his daughter.

Glancing at the picture, she could see so many resemblances the hair color was the same dark blonde color of his, her eyes had the same shape and from the picture look like the same blue-gray color as his. Even her smile and dimples resembled his. She would be shocked if the results came back negative.

In that moment, she made her decision. She grabbed her bag and packed all her belongings into it. She then called Piper and asked her to come pick her up. As she headed out of the room, she looked around. There was a framed picture of her and Marcus from the Christmas party, she walked over grabbed it and placed it in her bag. She'd make a copy of it and then send it back to him.

As she walked into the living room, waiting for Piper, she grabbed a piece of paper and pen and wrote a Dear John letter. She knew the mature thing to do would be to tell him to his face, but she also knew she couldn't do that. He would beg her to stay and she would crumble.

Just as she was finishing the note, she heard the doorbell ring. She took the note and laid it on the kitchen counter. She grabbed a coffee mug and placed it on the corner, so it wouldn't fly off and then grabbed her things and headed toward the door.

"Hey Pipe," she said as she opened the door.

"You sure you want to do this?" Piper asked as she took a bag from McKenzie's hand.

"No, but I don't think I can stay either."

"What does he say about all this?" McKenzie didn't answer, she just looked at her friend. "You didn't tell him you were leaving."

"I left a letter." McKenzie bit her lip.

"You left the poor man a Dear John letter?"

"I don't know if I say poor man." McKenzie trailed off.

"Come on, the man loves you."

"I know, and he would've have been able to talk me into staying, but I need to get away and figure this out."

"McKenzie," Piper paused as she locked the door behind her and they headed toward Piper's Ford Mustang. "What happened? What did he do or not do that is causing you to run?"

Piper opened the trunk and they put all her belongings in there before getting in the car and pulling out of the driveway. Once they got on the road, McKenzie told Piper everything. She broke down and told her that while she loved him, she just didn't think she could handle the fact that he had a child with another woman, while she had lost their child. Of course, Piper told her she was crazy. She understood, it would be hard, but if she really truly loved Marcus, she would find a way to make things work.

By the time they had arrived at McKenzie's apartment, she promised Piper she would think everything over. Regardless, she needed time away from Marcus to think. She also talked Piper into picking her up tomorrow and taking her to the doctor to get her cast removed. Marcus was supposed to take her, but under circumstances she knew she couldn't count on him.

After Piper left, she roamed around her apartment, putting her things up and then pulling out her laptop. As much as she tried to focus on her work, she couldn't. She finally shut down her computer and turned on the television. When that didn't work, she decided to take a nap. What she really wanted to do was go for a run, but with the stupid cast on, that was out of the question.

CHAPTER TWENTY-ONE

Marcus came home after a long day. Between practice and a double hitter, he was exhausted. What he really wanted to do was grab something to eat, strip down and go to bed with McKenzie cuddled up closed to him. However, he knew him and McKenzie needed to sit down and have a heart-to-heart, they had a lot to talk about.

Coach Anderson had called him into his office and let him know the blood test results had come back in and the child was definitely his. He still wasn't sure how that had happened, he had always been so careful. Other than McKenzie, he had never had unprotected sex. Regardless, he had a child now, a daughter. God must have a sense of humor to give him a daughter after the way he had treated women, including the mother of his child. He felt bad that he couldn't even remember Holly. He was a pig, no doubt about it.

"Kenz," Marcus called as he opened the door. It was quiet, too quiet. Normally, McKenzie had dinner going when he came home, but the kitchen was empty. He pulled out his phone to look and see if he missed a call or a text from her. Nothing. Maybe she was taking a nap. He headed back to the bedroom, she wasn't there either. He tried calling her, but the phone went straight to voicemail. He started to look around and noticed her hairbrush and other items were not on the dresser. He opened the drawers and the closet, all her stuff was gone.

"Shit!" He pulled his phone out and tried calling her again, "McKenzie, Baby, please call me back. Talk to me, please. I love you."

"Fuck! I need a drink," he grumbled to himself as he headed into the kitchen. He grabbed a beer out of the refrigerator and then glanced at the counter and saw a piece of paper with his name folded up under a coffee mug. He slowly reached out and grabbed the letter and then opened it.

Marcus,

I'm so sorry. I thought I could do this, but I can't. I love you with all my heart, but I can't do this. I wish you the

best.

McKenzie

"Fuck!" Marcus slid down the cabinet until he was sitting on the floor and buried his face in his hands. He sat there for thirty minutes or so nursing his beer when he heard a banging on his door. He stood up, downed the rest of his beer, grabbed another beer and then headed toward the door.

As he opened his door, he looked out to see Braxton and Tex standing on the other side of the door. He just stood and looked at them.

"Are you going to let us in?" Braxton asked as he handed him a box.

"What's this?" Marcus took the box.

"Well if you don't know what it is, that would explain how you keep getting girls pregnant."

"Fuck you, Braxton!" Marcus turned around and threw the box on the sofa. "Why the hell are you handing me a box of condoms?"

"You missed it, right after you left, Coach Anderson called everyone together and threw a box of condoms at each player. He told us to make sure we used them and if we didn't know how to use them properly we needed to ask one of buddies to teach us. He didn't want to hear about any more unplanned pregnancies." Tex explained.

"That would be the box he sent to you." Braxton pointed to the box on the sofa.

"Shit! He can be an asshole sometimes." Marcus shook his head.

"Well, let's face it Marcus, within six weeks," Tex paused. "Hell, less than six weeks you've had two unplanned pregnancies pop up. Grant it the pregnancies happened a little over two years apart from each other, but still."

"Fuck! I didn't even think about that," Marcus shook his head, "I guess I do look like a screw-up. Hell, it's probably a good thing I am retiring after this year or they would be trading my ass for sure."

"How are you holding up?" Braxton inquired as he glanced around the apartment from the door.

"You know?" Marcus questioned him.

"Yeah. I just got off the phone with Kendall a little while ago. She had just gotten off the phone with McKenzie."

"Do you also know that the child is definitely mine? The blood tests came back positive."

"I didn't know that, but McKenzie felt confident

she was after seeing the picture of your daughter in your room."

"My daughter," Marcus sighed, "What am I going to do?" He asked as he finally opened the door wide enough to allow his friends to come in."

"First, you're going to get your butt over McKenzie's place and talk to her," Tex said as he walked over to the refrigerator to grab a beer. He opened the fridge, grabbed two and threw one to Braxton. He looked down on the floor and saw the letter and leaned down to picked it up, "So this is the Dear John letter?"

"The what?" Marcus asked.

"A Dear John letter, a break-up letter. Piper told me she had written you one." He glanced at the letter, "I had to ask her what a Dear John letter was myself."

"Oh, great, so there is a name for this," Marcus shoved his hands through his hair and then glanced at Tex. "You talked to Piper? I didn't realize y'all were that close."

"Yeah, we talk every now and then."

"Every now and then, you just meet a week ago."

"Okay, we've talked a few times this week." Tex shook his head, "That's not the point though," he continued. "She's worried about McKenzie, so she called me. She felt like McKenzie needed to stick around and talk to you, but she also understood why she left. She's scared." Tex explained.

"Scared? Of what? Me?" Marcus probed.

"She has so much shit going through her head right now," Braxton spoke up, "According to Kendall, she's scared she'll lose you to your child. She's also scared she can never give you a child and even if she can, your first child was with another woman, not her. She's scared you'll leave her to go to San Diego to be with your child or that you'll deny your child to be with her. To top it all off, she still blames herself for the accident and losing the baby."

"What the hell?" Marcus looked at Braxton.

"Her head is all over the place. She's pretty fucked up right now, which is why I am sure she felt like she needed to get away." Braxton continued. "Listen, for what it is worth, I don't think it's so much the child as the timing. You're both trying to get on with your lives after losing the baby and now you have a child and it's not hers. She kind of got left out of that scenario. It's a lot to take in. I think bottom line, she is scared of getting hurt."

"That's some pretty deep shit. You come up with all that on your own?" Tex asked.

"Shit no! That was Kendall speaking, but after she said all that, it made sense."

"Regardless," Tex turned his attention back to Marcus, "the one consensus we got from both Piper and Kendall, and even this letter," he held the letter up, "is that she still loves you."

"You need to fight for her and don't let her say no," Braxton interjected. "You two have been through hell and back together, you cannot walk away now, and you cannot let her walk away now."

"What am I supposed to do?" Marcus asked, tears forming in his eyes, "I can't force her to come back to me."

"Go to her apartment. Don't leave until she talks to you or calls the police on you. The longer she is alone, the more time she has to think about things, which is not good." Tex commented.

"Last thing you want to do is allow a woman to sit alone and brood over things. It never ends well." Braxton commented, "I didn't go after Kendall when I should have, and it was ten years before we found each other again. Don't let ten years go by. Go to her now, we'll finish our beers and then lock up," he nodded toward Tex.

"Okay," Marcus stood and grabbed his keys. "Wish me luck, I'm going need it."

"Luck!" Braxton and Tex replied in unison as they raised their beers toward him, he half-grinned and darted out the door.

CHAPTER TWENTY-TWO

McKenzie woke up from her nap to a banging on the door. It took her a moment to wake up and adjust. Once she realized what was going on, she quietly snuck up to the door with her cell phone in hand. She already had plugged in 911 and was waiting see who was banging at her door before she hit send. As she peered through the peephole she saw Marcus and relaxed some.

"Come on McKenzie, open the door. I know you are in there."

There was no way he could know she was in there. She had been asleep in her room and then quietly moved into the living room and looked through peephole. She hadn't replaced her car, so he couldn't claim that he had seen her car in the parking lot.

"Kenz, Baby, please open up. Let's talk about this. Please."

McKenzie went back and forth trying to decide what to do. At one point she placed her hand on the door knob to open it, but then changed her mind. She finally slid down the door and sat with her back against it. She hoped Marcus would eventually give up and head back home.

"I'm not going anywhere McKenzie," he said as if he could read her thoughts. She then heard him slid down the door and felt the door jolt some as he plopped down on the ground.

McKenzie quietly pulled herself up and headed to her room. As soon as she made it in there she shut the door, laid across the bed and cried into her pillow. When she felt like she couldn't cry anymore, she got up and took a shower.

She couldn't get Marcus out of her head. The fact that he was sitting outside her door, didn't help any. She washed her hair and then took the soap and began running her hands up and down her body. She couldn't help but think of the last time she was in the shower with Marcus. She cupped her breasts and gently massaged them as Marcus had done. She then began pulling at her nipples using her forefinger and thumb. She then moved her hands slowly down her stomach and down to her womanhood. Slowly she inserted her fingers and then began thrusting them in an out moaning, "Marcus," as she sent herself into an orgasm.

She was going to miss the sex. Sex with him was better than any she had ever had. She was going to miss him, but things were too complicated for them. She pulled herself out of the shower and wrapped herself in a towel. She went back to the door and looked out the peephole expecting him to be gone, but when she looked through the hole, she could see his legs. He was obviously still sitting against the door, his legs straight out. She shook her head and then headed back to her room.

She pulled out her laptop and finished up her work, sent it off and then went to bed. She tossed and turned most of the night, struggling to get any sleep. She wondered if Marcus was still out there or if he had finally given up and went home.

Before McKenzie knew it, her alarm was going off. Piper would be there soon to drive her to the doctor. She was excited that she was finally going to get the cast off. She knew she would most likely have to have a removable cast, but at least she could take that off and give her leg a break.

She had quickly gotten dressed and gone into the kitchen to make herself a coffee to go when her phone pinged alerting her to a text message.

Piper: I'm here, but I'm not the only one.

McKenzie looked at the image Piper had sent along with her text. Marcus laid stretched out in front of her threshold. He had taken his shirt off and was using it as a pillow.

McKenzie: Shit! He's still there. Is he asleep?

Piper: Out like a light.

McKenzie: Don't wake him. I'm going to try and sneak out.

Piper: You need to talk to him. I mean he slept on the hard
floor waiting for you all night.

McKenzie: If he's still here when we get back from the doctor I will.

Piper: Okay, but I'm going to tell you what McKenzie, if
he wasn't so hung up on you, I would snatch him up in a

heartbeat.

McKenzie: I'll be out in a minute.

McKenzie didn't respond to Piper's last text. She wanted to text her back and tell her she could have him, but the truth was the thought of him with anyone else was not something she could bare. As much as she hated to admit it, that might be part of the problem with him having a child with another woman. Yes, she knew he had been with other women, but this was just proof. She would deal with her screwed up emotions later, for now, she needed to get to the doctor.

McKenzie made her to-go coffee and quietly headed toward the front door. She slowly opened it as not to wake Marcus. After handing her coffee mug to Piper, she placed one hand on the door frame and slowly crawled over him. She then carefully reached for the door knob and quietly shut the door and then quickly and as stealthy as she could with the cast on, walked down the hallway and rounded the corner with Piper right on her tail.

"You didn't lock the door," Piper whispered handing her the coffee mug.

"It was hard enough shutting the door. I was scared I would wake him if I tried to lock the door. Besides, it's not like he's going anywhere anytime soon."

"True, you've got your own personal guard dog."

"Guess you could say that," McKenzie chuckled.

As they got to the car, Piper stopped and looked at her friend.

"He loves you."

"I know he does, and I love him too."

"Then why are you being so stubborn."

"I just feel like it's one thing or another trying to pull us apart. Everything is so complicated," McKenzie paused and looked at Piper. "Is love really supposed to be this hard?"

"Yes! If it was easy, you wouldn't have break-ups and divorces, but if you love someone you fight for them," Piper opened her door and got in her car as McKenzie opened the passenger side and got in, "and" she continued, "he loves you. He is fighting for you right now. That is why he has been in the hallway all night and I'll bet he'll still be there when we get back. Talk to him and try and work this out. He's the best thing that has ever happened to you."

"Okay, like I said, if he's there when we get back, I'll talk to him."

"He will be." Piper grinned and pulled out of the parking lot.

◆ ◆ ◆

Several hours and a few stops later, Piper pulled back into the parking lot of McKenzie's apartment complex.

"Looks like he's still here," Piper pointed toward Marcus' car."

"Yep," McKenzie sighed, "would it be too much to hope he's still asleep."

"Yep." Piper grinned. "Do you need help with your groceries?"

'No, I'll be fine." McKenzie had asked Piper to stop by the grocery store on the way home from the doctor. Since her accident, she hadn't been home long enough to replenish her food. She only gotten enough to get by for a couple of days until she could plan out her meals for the week. "It'll be a lot easier now that I don't have the cast on."

"Take it easy on him, and call me later." Piper grinned as McKenzie grabbed the last of her grocery bags and shut the door. Piper pulled away as McKenzie entered the front lobby.

McKenzie rounded the corner of the hallway and saw Marcus sitting up against her door with a pizza box and sodas beside it. He glanced up at her and half-grinned.

She walked over to her door and looked at Marcus.

"You seem to be in my way," she commented.

"Yeah," he smiled, "I figured it's the only way in or out, eventually I would catch you. You need help with the groceries?"

"No, I got it. I think I can handle a few bags."

"McKenzie, please talk to me."

"Do you got any pizza left?" She eyed the pizza box.

"Yeah," he grinned.

"What kind?"

"Cheese"

"You like the Meat Lovers."

"Yeah, but you like cheese," he smiled at her as she looked him over, "and I got this," he held up a soda.

"A Mountain Dew?" McKenzie rolled her eyes and sighed. "Come on in, bring the pizza and the Mountain Dew."

Marcus didn't have to be told twice, he jumped up, Mountain Dew and pizza box in hands. "Where are your keys, I'll unlock the door."

"Door is unlocked."

"You left your door unlocked?"

"Well, it was hard to lock it with you laying across the threshold," she smirked. "Besides, I figured I had my own personal guard dog watching the door. It would be safe. However, I am glad to see you put your shirt back on. I'm not sure what my neighbors would think of a half-naked man lying in front of my door."

Marcus chuckled as he opened the door and let her in.

CHAPTER TWENTY-THREE

After Marcus made a quick run to the restroom to relieve himself and brush his teeth with the extra toothbrush McKenzie had, he returned to the living room and sat down on the sofa next to McKenzie who was eating a slice of pizza.

"Feel better?" She asked him as he sat down.

"Much better, thanks,' he grinned. "I was scared to go to the restroom because I didn't want to miss you and I know my breathe had to be bad since I hadn't brushed my teeth since I left the clubhouse last night."

"You brush your teeth at the clubhouse?"

"Yeah, after playing in the dirt, it's all in my teeth and mouth. It feels nasty, so I always shower and brush my teeth before I head out."

"Guess that's why your mouth always minty fresh when I kiss you after a game."

"Yeah, that would be why," Marcus paused and looked at her, "I could use some of that kissing now."

"Marcus," she began.

"I know," he half-grinned. "You got your cast off." He glanced down at her leg propped on the wooden coffee table.

"Yeah, finally."

"I thought you were going to have to wear one of those removable cast."

"The doctor said I was healing fine. He didn't see

any need for me to move to a walking cast as long as I promised to take it easy and not go overboard."

"I bet it's all tensed up from being in the cast for so long."

"Yeah, a little. I'll probably go get some ice and put it on it in a little bit."

"Here, let me see your foot," Marcus gently took it, along with her other leg and turned her around where her feet were now on his lap and her back was resting against the side of the sofa.

"Marcus," she looked at him, "What are you doing?"

"I'm going to massage your feet while we talk." He figured massaging her feet would be good for her and help him too, it would keep his hands busy and hopefully hide the nervousness he felt right now. He knew this talk could mean a reunion between the two of them or the end of the best thing he has ever known.

"Marcus," what started out as a complaint quickly turned into a moan as Marcus hit just the right spot. He knew exactly what he was doing.

"Relax, Baby," he pulled her foot up and kissed it.

"That's gross, I haven't washed that foot in since it went into the cast."

"There is not one part of you that is gross Baby, but I'll go get a warm cloth in a little bit and wash it up. Maybe a little lotion too, it does stink," he laughed.

"Shut up!" she chuckled.

At least he had her laughing he thought. "So, Baby," he began. He knew they just needed to jump into this and get everything out in the open. "I got your letter. It tore my heart apart."

"I'm sorry, I should've told you in person. It's just," she paused, "I had to get out of there, I had to think."

"I know," Marcus paused. "Talk to me and let me know what is going on in that pretty little head of yours."

"Did you get the results back?" She asked changing the subject.

"Yeah, she's definitely mine."

"So, what do you plan to do about it?"

"I don't know, I wanted to talk to you about it because you are my life. I want you in it. Whatever decision I make I want you to be a part of it because hopefully it will affect both of our lives," he paused for a moment. "I do know that I want to be a part of her life somehow, after all she is my daughter."

"Maybe you should try and work it out with her mother, so she can have a real family."

"I don't love her mother. Hell, I don't even remember her mother." He pushed on the palm of her feet with his thumbs realizing that was probably not the best thing to say.

"That's not helping your case," McKenzie cocked her head at him.

"I'm just saying, there is nothing there. That wouldn't be fair to her, her mother, me or you. You are the one I love, you are the one I want to marry. Seeing a loving marriage between us would be much better for her than a forced marriage where there is no love."

"This woman gave you your first child, and I lost your child. Why the hell would you want to be with me?"

"I love you and you need to quit blaming yourself," he sighed. "This may not be the time, but I really think maybe we should go see a therapist to help us get over this."

"We or me?"

"I think you are having a hard time dealing with it," Marcus carefully tried to think about what he was saying beforehand. He could see this blowing up in his face. "Your struggling with this, McKenzie, you know it, I know it, our family and friends know it. I think the timing of finding out about Emma sucks. We haven't had time to really grieve over the loss of our child and then another woman comes and throws a child at me. I know how that must make you feel," McKenzie puts her hand up and stops him mid-sentence and pulls her legs into her sitting Indian style. Marcus tenses as she pulls away from him."

"You don't know shit about how that makes me feel."

"Your right, I don't. Tell me please, tell me how it makes you feel."

McKenzie looked at him and then lowered her eyes, "It makes me feel inferior. I can't give you a child, but she can."

"McKenzie, the doctor said you could still have kids. I've told you before, I'm willing to start whenever you are. Hell, we can start tonight."

"Stick that dick back in your pants, because there ain't no sex happening here tonight."

"Ain't no sex, huh?"

"Do you really think right now is the time to correct my grammar?"

"No, I'm sorry, just a nervous reaction."

"Nervous, what are you nervous about?"

"McKenzie, you're kidding right? I'm scared to death you're going to walk away from me. I scared I'm going to lose the best thing that ever happened to me because of a stupid mistake I made more than four years ago."

"How can you say a child is a stupid mistake?"

"I'm not saying the child is a mistake. The truth is, I haven't even meet her and I've fallen in love with her. I'm saying the act that came before her was a mistake." Marcus ran his hands through his hair and then looked back up. "McKenzie, be honest, if I had known about Emma all along, if I had a four-year-old daughter when we first meet, would it have changed the way you felt about me."

"No," she shook her head, "I'm scared Marcus. I'm scared I'm going to be the one left behind, alone and hurt when this is all done and said."

"McKenzie, no," Marcus pulled himself off the sofa and went and bent down on his knees in front of her. "I will never intentionally do something to hurt you. I can't say I won't ever forget a birthday or not notice a new hairstyle, or say or do something stupid, but I will never cheat on you, lie to you, hide things from you, or make an important decision without including you. You are the most important person to me, well one of two important people now. I love you," he paused, "and I want you to go with me to San Diego to meet Emma. I want you to go as my fiancée and we can present a united front to Holly. I'm not asking you to go to flaunt another woman in front of Holly, but I'm asking you to go as my fiancée because this isn't just about me, it's about us. You have as much say as Holly or I do in this."

"Fiancée?"

"Yes, marry me McKenzie. I've wanted to propose for a while, but there never seemed to be a right moment," Marcus brought her hands to his lips and kissed her knuckles. "This may not be the right moment either, but to hell with it. I love you McKenzie Harper and I would be honored if you would be my wife. Please say yes."

McKenzie looked at Marcus, tears gathered in her eyes. At first, she didn't say anything. Marcus' heart started beating faster, his nerves were on edge and he could feel sweat starting to bead up on his forehead.

"Yes," McKenzie whispered.

"Yes?" Marcus raised his eyebrows.

"Yes. Yes, I'll marry you Marcus Hunter." She said as her eyes lit up and a smile broke across her face.

Marcus jumped up and pulled McKenzie off the sofa as he gathered her in his arms. "You have just made me the happiest man alive." He pulled her in tighter and leaned down crashing his lips to hers. As he pulled his lips from her, he looked her in the eye, "I've got a ring for you at the house. It was my grandmother's. I'd be honored if you would wear it. I know she would have liked you if she had meet you."

"I would be honored to wear her ring," she leaned over and kissed him.

CHAPTER TWENTY-FOUR

After a night of making love, McKenzie woke to find Marcus' legs and arms wrapped around her so tightly there was no way she was moving from the bed without waking him. She had a feeling his sub-conscious, or maybe even his conscience mind was scared she would run again.

"Marcus, Baby," she said as she rubbed her fingers up and down his muscular forearm.

"Ummm" he muttered.

"I need to go to the restroom and your kind of wrapped around me."

"Ummm," he muttered again, but loosened his grip.

McKenzie kissed his arm as he started to pull it away to release her and then pulled her naked body out of the bed. She leaned down and grabbed Marcus' t-shirt on the way into the bathroom.

McKenzie took her time freshening up and brushing her teeth. She then threw Marcus' t-shirt on and headed back out into her bedroom. She figured she would make breakfast, but when she came out of the bathroom, Marcus obviously had different plans. He was sitting up in the bed, still naked, beckoning her to him as he patted the bed next to him.

McKenzie slowly moved over to the bed and crawled up onto it.

"Love seeing you in my t-shirt," Marcus gruffly

commented, "but it's gotta go." He grabbed the hem of the shirt and yanked it off.

"You didn't get enough sex last night?"

"I can never get enough of you," he pressed his hardness up against her stomach as he pulled her to him.

She moved her hands down his chest until she reached his cock.

"You know this is a dangerous weapon you have here, right?" McKenzie asked as she wrapped her hand around his cock and caressed the length of his erection.

"I guess you can say that," he grinned.

"You know we didn't use a condom at all last night."

"I know, I've got some in my wallet if you want to grab them."

"I kind of liked you barebacking it last night. It felt good."

"I kind of liked it too."

"Besides, if we didn't wear one last night, it's not going to make a difference this morning."

"True," Marcus paused, "have you started back on your birth control pills?"

"No, I made an appointment with my OBGYN when we got back from Atlanta, but he didn't have any available appointments until next week."

"He?"

"Yes, he."

"Maybe you should look for a female doctor."

"Why Marcus Hunter, are you jealous of my OBGYN?"

"I just don't want another man down there. I

want to be the only man to see what you have."

"So, you prefer a woman down there?"

"Yeah," he smirked, "in fact, if you..."

"Marcus," she warned him, "don't finish that sentence."

Marcus laughed then pulled her down under him. "Just you and me Baby, no one else." McKenzie pulled herself up and began nipping at his ears. "Your killing me, Kenz."

"What ya going to do about it?" She whispered into his ear and then drew it into her mouth and began sucking on it.

"Shit, Kenz! I didn't think you could orgasm from someone sucking on your ears, but I think I'm about to blow." He began moving his hand down her body until he reached her clit. As soon as he started rubbing it, she let out a moan and released his ear. He took that opportunity and quickly moved down and began flicking her clit with his tongue.

"Unfair move," McKenzie moaned.

"All's fair in love and war Baby," he stopped to look at her before returning to the invasion between her lips.

"Marcus, I need you inside me," she begged.

"Ummm," he teased her as he inserted his fingers into her and began thrusting them in and out of her, "not yet."

One more hard thrust and McKenzie began to writhe and groan as she hit an orgasm. Marcus didn't give her time to come down from her climax before he was positioning himself over her and then slowly inserted the head of his cock, teasing her he pushed in a little and then pulled back out. He penetrated her a little further before pulling out again. Slowly he penetrated her again, this time a little further, but McKenzie was done with his teasing, so she wrapped her legs around his waist, placing her feet on his ass, she pressed up toward him and pushed down with her feet.

"Marcus, not sure what the hell you are doing, but pick up the pace or I'm going to get myself off."

Marcus laughed and then began thrusting into her until she hit her climax and he followed right behind her, releasing all his seed into her and then collapsing on her. McKenzie wrapped her arms around him and began rubbing her hands up and down his back. As soon as he was able to pull himself back together he rolled over and laid beside her.

"Let's go take a shower," Marcus whispered breathlessly into McKenzie's ear.

"Haven't had enough yet?"

"Like I said before, I can never get enough of you." Marcus replied as he sat up and pulled himself off the bed reaching his hand out for hers. She reached out and took his hand as he pulled her up toward him, wrapping her legs around him, he walked them into the bathroom.

Marcus headed into the kitchen and began making breakfast as McKenzie got dressed and packed a bag to head back to Marcus' place. They still had a lot to talk about and McKenzie was determined that they were not leaving her apartment until they had talked things through.

McKenzie headed into the living room and laid her bag down by the door and then strolled over to the kitchen. She pulled up a barstool and sat down at the kitchen bar. "What can I do to help?"

"Nothing, I've got it covered," Marcus replied as he handed her a cup of coffee.

"Marcus, what are you going to do about Emma?"

"Well, that's where I wanted to talk to you. Like I said before, this includes you too since you'll be my wife and Emma's step-mother."

"Wow, I hadn't thought about that," McKenzie's mind started racing as she started playing with her ring finger, even though Marcus hadn't put a ring on yet.

"It'll be oaky, Baby. We're going to work it out together," Marcus took her both her hands in his and began rubbing circles on the back of it, reading her mind again. *How did he do that?*

Marcus turned back around and slid some pancakes on two plates along with some sausage patties. He grabbed the syrup out of the cabinet, the two plates of foods and placed them on the kitchen bar. "Hope pancakes are okay. You didn't have a lot of breakfast options here."

"Yeah, I haven't been here much in the past month." She responded as he turned and grabbed two forks and his coffee mug.

"We can throw this apartment into the mix of something else we need to talk about."

"What about my apartment?"

"Do you really need to hold on to it if we are getting married? My townhome is a little bigger and it's paid for. I think we should live there. I know we're not married yet, but I would really like it if you go ahead and move in."

"Marcus, you're here one more week and then you're on the road. Do you really think right now is the time for me to move out?"

"Yeah, it'll save money.

"Do we need to be worrying about money? Did you spend all your money on your Porsche and fancy high-rise condo?"

"No, money is fine, smart-ass," he smirked, "but if I'm retiring, the money won't be coming in like it has been. There is no need for us to spend money unnecessarily, so I think your apartment and my condo in Atlanta should go. I'll talk to a realtor as soon as I get back to Atlanta."

"You still have the rest of the season to go, where are you going live if you sell your condo?"

"I'll crash at Tex' place or with Braxton and Kendall. I can spend some time with my soon to be nephew and niece."

"Okay, I'll talk to the apartment leasing office this week," she looked over at him, "so that was the easy conversation, back to Emma."

"Yeah, so here's the thing, I'm flying out Thursday to go to San Diego and meet Emma and talk to Holly. I plan on being back by Saturday. I can finish out our last week of spring training down here before heading back to Atlanta to start the official season. However, Coach did say if I needed to stay longer it would be fine, just be back in Atlanta a week from Sunday for the first official game of the season," he paused for a moment as McKenzie sat and looked at him, not sure what to day, "so," he continued, "I have two things I want to address here. The first one being, I want you to go with me to San Diego. Like I told you before, I want us to stand as a united front. I want Holly to know that while I will be there for Emma, you are my future, not her. Plus, I think it's important that Emma meet you since you will be part of her life and vice versa. To top it off, and this is the selfish part of me, I know, but I need you there with me, by my side. I need you."

"The second thing," McKenzie finally spoke.

"What?"

"You said there was two things," McKenzie responded, she could tell Marcus was confused as she hadn't addressed the first thing yet.

"Oh, that goes back to the living situation, I want to get you moved out of the apartment and settled into our place before I head back to Atlanta."

"Okay." McKenzie looked down at her plate, cut a bite of pancake off and played with it moving it around the plate.

"McKenzie, Baby. What are you thinking?" Marcus' nerves were working overtime.

"That your right, Emma needs to meet me, and I need to meet her, so I'll go. I'm also going for selfish reasons to."

"What would that be?"

"I want to meet this woman who gave you your first child. I also want her to know that you are mine, so she better not even think about trying to seduce you."

"I like that your claiming me," a smile spreading

from ear to ear formed across his face.

"Don't get too cocky," she jabbed him in the shoulder.

"Okay, so change of plans," he began as she cocked her head looking at him. "We go back to my place and drop of your bag and I'll get ready for practice. Then you take the SUV and meet me over at the UHAUL store and we will get some boxes and tape. You head back to your place and start packing. I'll head over after the game and help you. If we do a little each day, maybe we can get you moved into the town home before I have to head back to Atlanta."

"What if I want to go to the game?"

"Then come on, Baby," he smirked. "You know I love having you there."

CHAPTER TWENTY-FIVE

Over the next two days, with the help of some of Marcus' teammates, in between practices and games they managed to get her apartment packed and moved over to Marcus' town home. The boxes had all been placed in the garage until they had time to go through them and figure out where everything would go.

Marcus figured he would need to go through the townhome and pack some of his things up, to make room for McKenzie's things. He also felt like they may need to think about selling the townhome and purchasing a house. He had a two-bedroom townhome that would be fine for when Emma came to stay with him. That was one thing he planned on negotiating with Holly. She may have a problem with him bringing her across the state, hell across the country, but damn it, she was his daughter too and Holly would have to deal with it.

So, a two-bedroom townhome would be fine for him, McKenzie and Emma, but what if him and McKenzie had more kids, which was something he wanted and a high possibility with the way they had been going lately. And wouldn't that beat all, him having to tell Coach about a third unplanned pregnancy all within a six-week time span. Coach would have a cow. Hell, he would just tell him, they planned it this time, they were officially engaged after all.

First thing Marcus did when they walked into the house after leaving McKenzie's apartment two days ago was put his grandmother's engagement ring on her finger. He didn't want to waste anytime placing claim on his woman.

McKenzie was so appreciative of the ring and stared down at the unique qualities it held. The one diamond carat was set in a handmade 1940's sterling silver ring with leaf designs throughout it. While the diamond was not the largest, the ring was such a unique design and the sentimental value associated with it brought tears to McKenzie's eyes and filled Marcus' heart with more love, if that was even possible.

Marcus was bringing a box of McKenzie's clothes into the bedroom where McKenzie was packing a bag for San Diego. She was oblivious to the fact that he had entered the room. She was putting a shirt into the bag when she stopped and put her hand out in front of her admiring her ring finger, his heart soared as he watched her, and he saw a smile form on her beautiful, flawless face.

"Here, Baby. He's another box of clothes," he announced himself. "Do we need to unpack these boxes before we go, or do you have what you need for the trip?"

"I'm good," she jumped as she looked up at him.

"Sorry, didn't mean to scare you," he apologized as he sat the box in the corner and then walked over and pressed a kiss against her soft red lips.

"You're good. I was just deep in thought," she smiled. "I think we are all packed."

"Good," he replied as his phone pinged and he

looked at the text message that came through.

"You ready to go? We need to leave soon if we are going to make the flight. Braxton and Tex are waiting outside for us. They are going to drop us off at the airport.

"You got both of them to take us the airport? Couldn't just one of them have done it?"

"If you haven't figured it out yet, Baby, we do everything together. Hell, they would be going to San Diego with us if Coach would let them."

"As long as they stay out of our bedroom." She grinned.

"I draw the line there," he chuckled as he grabbed the bags and headed toward the door. McKenzie followed with her purse, laptop bag and a gift bag.

"What's in the bag?" Marcus nodded toward the gift bag.

"A doll for Emma," she grinned. "I figured it might be nice if her dad gave her a gift when he first meets her," she winked at him.

"Dad," he paused. "That's going to take some getting used to," he shook his head. "What kind of doll?" He wasn't sure why he was asking, like he knew anything about dolls.

"It's an AG Doll," she replied as he looked at her like she was speaking gibberish, "They are really cool, you can buy dolls that look like you and you can get matching clothes. I bought her a doll with wavy dark blonde hair like hers. She's in a ballerina costume because I noticed Emma had on a leotard and ballet shoes in the picture you have, so I figured she took ballet. I also bought her a softball outfit for the doll, complete with a glove, hat and catcher's mask," Marcus' eyes lit up, "and a matching sundress for her and the doll."

"You are too much," he pulled her in, still holding the bags and kissed her passionately.

"We gotta go. Your posse is waiting for us," McKenzie moved away hesitantly.

As the airplane landed at LAX, Marcus could feel knots in his stomach starting to form. He wasn't sure why he was so nervous. He was going to meet a four-year-old little girl, his four-year-old little girl. That would be why he was so nervous. What if he couldn't do this? He didn't know how to be a father, what if he screwed this up? What if he screwed her up? He could feel the panic setting in and sweat beads forming on his forehead.

"Are you okay?" McKenzie asked as she looked over at him.

"Yeah, why?" his voice shaking. He looked straight ahead, scared to look McKenzie in the eyes for fear she could see right through him.

"Because you look green."

"What?" he turned and looked at her quizzically.

"You look like you want to throw-up."

Marcus looked her in the eyes and then took in a deep breath. "What if I'm not a good father, what if I screw everything up? What if I screw her up?" he lowered his head ashamed of himself.

"Marcus, look at me," McKenzie put her fingers under his chin and pulled his face up until he was looking her in the eye.

"The fact that you are worried about it, tells me you are going to be a good father," she leaned over and kissed him on the cheek. "I've seen you with Jax and Josie, you are great with them, those kids adore you. You're going to be just as great with Emma and she is going to love you because you are her daddy."

"I love you," Marcus leaned over and planted his lips on McKenzie's, feeling just a little more relaxed.

"I love you too," she smiled and then stood up and took his hand. "Now let's go meet your daughter."

CHAPTER TWENTY-SIX

After waiting in line for a rental car and then getting settled into their hotel, Marcus and McKenzie pulled up to two-story run-down apartment complex. The grounds were obviously not taken care of as overgrown weeds were prominent throughout. Looking around, Marcus noticed the heavy black bars on the doors and windows.

"Please tell me the GPS is wrong and this is not where my daughter lives," Marcus' knuckles turned white as he clutched the steering wheel.

"Marcus, listen to me," McKenzie turned and faced Marcus as he pulled into a parking place. "We don't know what we will see inside, but don't go in half-cocked ready to ream her out. We don't know what she has had to go through as a single mom. Let's go in, access the situation and then decide what to do."

"I know, what I'm doing. I'm buying her a damn house to get my daughter out of this area."

"Stay calm and let's think of a way to approach that situation without being accusatory."

"God, I'm glad you are with me," Marcus looked over at McKenzie and gave her a half-grin and then open his door and stepped out of the rental sedan. He walked around the car, open the door for McKenzie as she reached in the back for the gift bag. McKenzie took his outstretched hand and let him pull her out ofthe car. Once he shut the door, they walked hand-n-hand to apartment 212.

Marcus knocked on the door as McKenzie squeezed his hand, letting him know she was there to support him.

"Yes," Marcus heard someone say on the other side of the door.

"I'm looking for Holly Wright," he yelled through the door.

"Who are you?" the voice inquired.

"Marcus Hunter, she's expecting me."

It got quiet and Marcus had wondered if whoever was at the door had walked off and was about to knock on the door again, but heard chains and locks being undone. The door opened and an older lady, stood in the doorway looking at a picture in her hand and then looking him up and down. She finally stepped aside and motioned for them to come in.

"Um, is Holly here?" He asked as he looked around the apartment. It was clean, but the ceiling had water stains throughout and the walls had dec-ade old wallpaper on it, half of it peeled off.

"Yeah, she's in her room, but there is something you should know," the lady responded as a dirty blonde little girl came out of the room, holding an old worn out doll.

The little girl looked over at McKenzie and then over at Marcus. She began sizing him up and down. Marcus breathed in deeply and then grabbed McKenzie's hand and squeezed it. He was in love. This little girl was his little girl and he wanted to run to her, grab her up and hug her tight. However, he was smart enough to know that would scare her, so he gave her time to take them in. She slowly walked up to them and Marcus dropped McKenzie's hand. Emma grabbed Marcus's hand and looked up to him.

"Daddy?" she asked.

"Um yeah," Marcus responded looking at McKenzie and then the older lady who had answered the door. She walked up to him and put her arms around him and gave him a big hug. Marcus wrapped his arms around her, picked her up and hugged her back as a tear fell down his check. He glanced over to McKenzie who had tears running down her face, as well as the older lady.

"McKenzie and I brought you something," Marcus told her as he walked over to the worn put sofa and sat down with her in his lap.

"A present?" she asked excitedly.

"Yes," Marcus chuckled as he handed her the gift bag.

Emma took the gift bag, crawled out of his lap and sat down on the floor to open it. She threw the tissue paper out and pulled out the doll. She let out a squeal then jumped up and crawled up in Marcus' lap with the doll in hand, still in the box.

"Open," she said handing him the doll and then crawled back down and went back to the bag and pulled out the clothes. She had him open those too as she took the doll from him and hugged it tight.

"She needs a name, what do you want name her?" McKenzie asked as she came over and sat down beside Marcus.

"I'll ask Mommy," she said as she grabbed the doll and ran back down the hall.

"Where is Holly? Why isn't she in here? And who

are you? Are you her mother? How did Emma know I was her dad?" Marcus shot off one question after another looking at the older lady.

"Okay, wow," the older lady answered. "Let me see if I can answer all those questions. First of all, Emma knew you were her dad because Holly has been trying to prepare her for your visit." She responded as she handed him a picture.

"Oh my God, I remember her," he responded as he looked at the picture of him and Holly. It was after the game almost five years ago which put them into the World Series. He had drunk a little more than he should have, but he still knew he had worn a condom. He was religious about it. He also remembered that they went at it like rabbits, so maybe one time he forgot. He handed the picture to McKenzie who half-grinned. He knew this had to be hard on her. He would have to show her how much he appreciated it in more than words and sex. He would have to figure out something.

"You didn't remember her?" The lady asked.

"No," he shook his head in shame, "I use to be player, wasn't really a one-woman kind of man, until recently," he glanced over at McKenzie. "Who are you?" He looked back up to the lady.

"My name is Edith, but Emma calls me Edie. I am Emma and Holly's caregiver."

"Why does Holly need a caregiver and where is she?"

"Holly is sick."

"Sick, like the flu? Should we go get Emma out the room, she doesn't need to get sick."

"No, like leukemia."

"Oh," Marcus let pout a breath. "How bad?"

"She's in stage IV. She has gone through chemo, had a bone marrow transplant and has fought with everything she has, but her body is done fighting. She doesn't have much longer. That's why she contacted you. She wanted to know that Emma would be taken care of."

"So, if she hadn't gotten sick, she wouldn't have contacted me," Marcus ran his hands through his hair as McKenzie placed her hand on his thigh, again reassuring him that she was there for him.

"Probably not," Edith responded.

"I want to be mad about that, but if she's dying, I can't...," his thoughts trailed off. "What about family?"

"She doesn't have any. Her father was in the military and died when he was deployed. She was only twelve at the time. Her mother died last year of a heart attack."

"Wow, it had to be hard raising Emma on her own. I wish she would have contacted me sooner, like when she found out she was pregnant."

"Come on, let me take you to go see her," Edith headed toward the hallway. Marcus and McKenzie stood up and followed her down it.

CHAPTER TWENTY-SEVEN

As they approached the bedroom, Marcus froze in doorway. He looked over at Holly who was laying in the bed with a weak smile. She was looking at Emma who was showing her the new doll Marcus had given her. She had a do-rag wrapped around her head, an oxygen nasal tube in her nose and looked anorexic. If he hadn't had seen the picture Edith had shown him earlier, he would have never known who she was.

"Holly," Edith softly called her name.

She slowly turned her head and saw Marcus and McKenzie standing in the doorway. "Hey, Marcus," she weakly smiled.

"Hey," Marcus responded as he walked over to her and laid a kiss on her forehead.

"Emma, let's take your doll out to the living room and play with it," McKenzie suggested.

"Okay," Emma leaned over and kissed her mother, then jumped off the bed and ran over to McKenzie. She grabbed her hand and walked out the door with her. Edith followed behind shutting the door, leaving Marcus alone with Holly.

"I'm betting if I wasn't dying you would be yelling at me right now instead of kissing my forehead." Holly smirked.

"Probably," Marcus half-grinned as he pulled a chair up to the bed and sat down. "Holly, why didn't you tell me about Emma before now?"

"Honestly, I had planned on it." She looked away for a minute and then back to him, "I sabotaged the condoms, I thought if I got pregnant you would marry me."

"What do you mean you sabotaged the condoms?"

"If you recall, I put the condoms on you each time we had sex, I purposely popped holes in them, enough to cause leakage, but not enough you would know."

"Holy, shit," Marcus ran his hand through his hair trying not to yell. "I'm not going to yell, it won't do any good now."

"And you don't want to yell at a dying woman," Holly half-grinned.

"Nevertheless, " Marcus continued, not admitting to her that was the only reason he wasn't yelling, "I wouldn't have married you, but I would have taken care of Emma."

"I know, you're a good man Marcus."

"So, you were going to try and trap me. Why didn't you follow through with it?"

"I grew a conscience," she smirked, "I felt bad about it. I knew you were a player, you weren't ready to settle down and I didn't want to trap you with a kid."

"Well, regardless of what happened or why it happened, we now have Emma and we need to talk about her."

"Take her with you."

"What?"

"Take her home with you and McKenzie. I don't have long, I want to know she's taken care of and loved," Holly said with tears falling down her face, "will McKenzie love her?"

"Yeah," Marcus was at a loss for words, "she was actually the one who bought the doll and clothes. She noticed what she was wearing in the picture and bought her a ballerina doll because of it."

"Good. When are you two getting married?"

"We haven't set a date yet, we just recently got engaged."

"I want her to adopt Emma. She needs a mama and since I won't be here, I want McKenzie to be her mama."

"Holly," Marcus began, but wasn't really sure what to say.

"Marcus, don't, just listen," she stopped him, "Edith helped me pack Emma's stuff. Her birth certificate and other important papers are in the front of her suitcase.

"Is my name on the birth certificate?"

"Yes," she paused, "there is a big red boot box on the top shelf of my closet. Can you get it?"

Marcus stood up and walked over to the closet, grabbed the box and brought it to her.

"Open it," she said, with every breath getting weaker and weaker.

Marcus opened it and then sat it on the bed beside her.

"In this box are letters and videos for Emma. They are for important events in her life, her first date, her first heartbreak, getting her period," Marcus scowled, "losing her virginity,"

"Whoa, she's not going to lose her virginity," Marcus said.

"Good luck with that Dad," Holly chuckled, but

then began to cough.

Marcus grabbed the water off her nightstand and handed it to her.

"Thanks," she responded as she took the water, drank a sip and then handed the cup back to him, "If you can, find a place to put these, a place she knows where they are. As she gets older, she can go find them and get the letter or video she needs. If she knows where it is and it's something she is embarrassed to come to you about, then she can find the letter on her own. I labeled each one with the event. I began these letters and videos a year ago when I found out I was sick, I didn't know about McKenzie then, so I didn't know if she would have a woman to go to, so I tried to hit on all kinds of feminine issues and things a girl just wouldn't want to go to her dad about."

"Oh, stop," Marcus said trying not to think of his little girl as a woman.

Holly laughed, starting a coughing fit, so Marcus grabbed the water again.

"I also put my Mama's pearls in there. I want you to hold on to those and give them to her on her wedding day," tears started falling down her face.

"Holly," Marcus ran his hand through her hair. A clump feel came out in his hand and a shiver went down him as he dropped it down on the pillow beside her head, trying to hide it from her. She either didn't notice it or choose to ignore it.

"I know you and McKenzie are going to take care of her, but just knowing I won't be there for her first date, prom, her wedding and all the important events in her life, it's just hard. I want her to move on and be happy. I want McKenzie to be a mom to her, but please don't let her forget me." She pleaded as tears streamed down her face.

"I promise, I won't," Marcus continued to stroke her hair.

"Do you mind if I talk to McKenzie alone?" Holly asked.

"Sure, I'll go get her," he stood up, leaned over kissed her head and then headed out of the room.

"Marcus," she softly called as he got to the door.

"Please take Emma tonight. I don't want her to be here when I go to meet my maker."

Marcus nodded as he forced a smile for her.

CHAPTER TWENTY-EIGHT

McKenzie slowly walked into the living room carrying the red shoe box with the letters and videos, tears streaming down her face.

Marcus looked over at Edith and nodded at Emma. Understanding what he was saying, she went over to Emma and sat down next to her as Marcus stood up and walked over to McKenzie. He took the box from McKenzie and laid it on the table, then took her hand and led her outside to talk.

As he soon as the door shut, he leaned over and took his thumb running under her eyes to dry up the tears.

"You okay?"

"Yeah, I just..." McKenzie trailed off not sure what to say.

"I know, Baby," Marcus leaned down and kissed her cheek.

"That poor little girl,' McKenzie paused and looked at Marcus, "your poor little girl."

"Our poor little girl," Marcus corrected her.

"Yeah, our poor little girl," she looked up at Marcus, "she wants us to take her tonight."

"Yeah, she told me. Are you okay with that?"

"Yeah, I am," she nodded. "She told me she wants me to adopt her, she wants me to be her mom," McKenzie sobbed as she spoke those words.

"How do you feel about that?"

"I'd be more than happy to call that little precious little girl my daughter. I just hate that she's having to lose her mother in order for me to do that."

"I know. I hate it too."

"How are we going to keep the memory alive of someone I just met, and you really don't know either."

"I really don't know, I've wondered that same thing. I guess the letters and the pictures are the best we got." Marcus paused. "What am I going to tell her when she asks about mine and Holly's relationship, because you know in some point and time she will ask," he sighed, "What do I tell her? I can't very well tell her that her mother and I were a one-night stand and she's only here because her mother messed with the condom in order to get pregnant and try to trap me."

"What?" McKenzie's eyes were suddenly open wide.

"Oh, she didn't tell you that I guess."

"No, she didn't. Obviously, her plan worked as far as getting pregnant. Why didn't she follow through and try to trap you?"

"She said she grew a conscience."

"Wow!"

"Yeah."

Marcus and McKenzie talked a little bit longer about what they needed to do. McKenzie pointed out that the house was not conducive for a child and they would need to set a room up for her right away. Marcus put McKenzie on shopping duty. She was going to go online and see what she could go ahead and order and have delivered when they returned.

"So, when are we returning home? I mean we have Emma now and we don't know how long until Holly passes on. What are your thoughts?" McKenzie asked.

I don't know. I need to talk to Edith and see what, if anything has been done for funeral arrangements for when the time comes. She doesn't have any family from what I gather. I wouldn't even know who to contact," he paused and then with sadness in his eyes he looked McKenzie straight in her eyes, "I don't think she is going to last much longer. Her breathing was shallow and weak, " he sighed. "I haven't really seen anybody dying before, other than my grandmother, but she reminds me of how my grandmother was right before she died. If I thought there was any way she could survive, I would offer to pay her medical bills to get her the help she needed, but I just don't think she has that kind of time."

"I don't either. In fact, I would be surprised if she made it through the week. Truth be told, I think she was hanging on for you to get here. I think she wants to know Emma is going to be taken care of."

"Yeah, I kind of got the same feeling," Marcus responded as a growl rumbled from within him.

"Tell you what, it's past lunchtime, according to your stomach," she chuckled. "Why don't we take Emma to eat, maybe to the park and then for some ice cream, then we can regroup.

"Okay, that sounds like a plan. Let me talk to Edith before we head out." Marcus replied just as the door opened.

"I hate to interrupt, but I just went to check on Holly, she's gone." Edith said with tears in her eyes.

Marcus drew in a quick gasp of air. McKenzie

could see tears building in his eyes. Taking his hand in hers, she gave him a quick squeeze to let him know she was there for him. He squeezed back.

"Where's Emma?"

"She's playing in the living room," she paused and looked at Marcus, "she had gone back there to see Holly and came back and said she was asleep. I went back to check on her and she's gone."

"Who do we need to call?" McKenzie asked.

"I'm going to call 911. I wanted to give to time to get Emma out of here first, but other than that, there isn't anyone really to call. She has no family and her so called friends disappeared when things got rough."

"What a way to go, at least she had Emma," another sigh. "God, how am I going to tell Emma this?"

"Do you want me to talk to her?" McKenzie asked.

"No, I'll do it, but thanks," Marcus leaned over and kissed McKenzie's forehead.

"Tell her that her mom is an angel now and pull yourself together before you talk to her." McKenzie suggested.

"Okay, I guess I'll see what needs to be done about making arrangements."

"Holly already took care of that," Edith sniffled.

"What do you mean?"

"She already talked to the funeral home and set up arrangements to be cremated."

"That's awful, no one should have to plan their own funeral." McKenzie wrapped her arms around Marcus' waist.

"I wished I known earlier. I know I don't really know Holly that well, but she is the mother of my child. I would've done whatever I could to help her."

"I guess I should go talk to Emma." Marcus gave McKenzie a quick squeeze and she then slowly released her arms from around his waist.

Edith turned to head in. Marcus and McKenzie followed her in.

"I'm going to head to the back room and call 911," Edith commented as she walked on by.

Marcus went and sat Indian style down on the floor beside Emma. McKenzie stood back enough out of the way to give Marcus and Emma space, but close enough that Marcus knew she was there for him if needed.

"Hey, Princess," Marcus grinned at her. "What ya doing?"

"I'm changing her clothes, so we can wear the same dress." She said as she stood up and twirled around in the new dress she had just gotten. She had obviously changed into it while Marcus and McKenzie were outside talking.

"Oh, well you both look very pretty," he took her little hand in his as she twirled. "Come here squirt, I want to talk to you for a minute," he pulled her onto his lap.

"Yes, Daddy," she smiled. Marcus' heart melted just hearing her call him Daddy.

"You know Mommy's been in the bed a lot lately because she hasn't been feeling well."

"Yeah, she's been sick," she turned and looked at Marcus and began running her hands over his stubble. "She said one day the angels will come take her home with them and she won't be sick anymore."

"She told you that?"

"Yeah."

"Well sweetie," Marcus paused. "Those angels came down and took her home with them today."

"Mommy's with the angels?"

"Yeah, she's not sick anymore."

"Will I get to see her again?"

"Not for a long, long time."

"I going to miss my Mommy," the tears started welding up in her eyes.

"I know baby, but she'll always be with you, in your heart."

"Mommy said when the angels took her, I would go with you. Am I going with you now?"

"Yeah, baby. You're going with me and McKenzie now."

Emma pushed up off of Marcus and walked over to McKenzie. "Are you my mommy now?"

"Oh, baby," McKenzie leaned down until she was eye level with Emma. "I can never replace your Mommy. She loved you so much, but I'll be your stand in Mommy. I love you too and I'll try and be the best Mom I can be to you." Emma reached up and put her arms around McKenzie's neck and hugged her tight as she started to cry. McKenzie just wrapped her arms around her and let her cry.

"I'm going to miss my mommy."

"I know baby," McKenzie stood up, pulling Emma into her arms and holding her tight.

Edith came out of the back room with Emma's suit case and a bag. "The ambulance is on the way, so you might want to head on out with Emma."

"Okay, we will," Marcus responded as he stood up and then looked over to Emma. "Do you have any dolls, toys, pillow you want to take with you?

"Yeah, I want my pillow and Mr. Snuggles."

"I'll go with her and get what she needs." McKenzie responded as she slowly let Emma down and took her hand.

Emma lead McKenzie back to her room. Marcus watched them walk back and then walked over to Edith. "Do you think we can we get her ashes? I would like to put them at a cemetery near us, so Emma can go visit when she is older."

"It shouldn't be a problem. I'll text you the number of the crematorium, it's on Holly's phone. They can probably ship her ashes to you, so you don't have to worry about them traveling."

"Thanks," Marcus looked around. "What's going to happen to all her stuff?

"There is a women's shelter down the road. She asked me to donate all of her things to them."

"What about jewelry or family heirlooms, anything that will mean something to Emma when she is older?"

"Truth is, Holly sold almost everything she had to pay for medical, rent and food, so she really doesn't have much. There is a small box in Emma's suitcase with anything of value she had left. I also put some pictures of Holly and Emma in there. It would be nice if you could frame some of them and put them in her room."

"I'll do that. I don't want her to forget her mom."

"You're a good man, Marcus. I'm glad Emma has you and McKenzie."

"Thanks." Marcus looked up as McKenzie and Emma came down the hallway. McKenzie was carrying a pillow and a bag with some toys, including a big stuffed horse in Emma had her hands."

"Who's this?" Marcus asked leaning down and looking at the horse that was almost as big as Emma.

"Mr. Snuggles," she replied.

"Oh," he looked up at McKenzie, "I was expecting a teddy bear."

"Me too," she chuckled.

"Let's go before things get exciting around here," he motioned McKenzie and Emma out the door.

"Can we come back and help you with anything? Packing or whatever needs to be done?" Marcus stopped and looked at Edith.

"No, but thanks. The people from the women's shelter said they would send people over to pack it up. Thanks for the offer."

"Okay, we'll call if you need anything. My number is on Holly's phone." Edith nodded as Marcus started out the door. He stopped and looked at McKenzie and Emma near the car. "What about a car seat?"

"She doesn't have one. Holly sold her car for the money and just took the bus wherever she needed to go."

"Okay, guess that will be one of our first stops. I mean it, call if you need anything." He picked up the suitcase again as well as the red box full of letters and videos and headed toward the rental car.

CHAPTER TWENTY-NINE

"I can't believe you've got a kid now." Tex drawled as him and Braxton helped Marcus fix up the spare room for Emma.

"Have you talked to the in-laws yet?" Braxton asked.

"Yeah," Marcus rolled his eyes.

"Did he yell at you about keeping your dick in your pants again?"

"Yep," Marcus scowled as he screwed a nut and bolt into place on the white canopy bed he was putting together for Emma.

"McKenzie wanted to go to their house and talk to them in person, but we figured it would probably be best if we just told them over the phone instead of showing up with a kid.

"You know they will love Emma just like they love Jax and Josie." Braxton commented.

"I hope so, because they'll be the only grandparents Emma will have."

"I know Mr. Harper can be a hard ass, but Mrs. Harper keeps him grounded. He'll softened toward you once you and McKenzie are officially married. Just don't get her pregnant before then."

"How are things going with Piper?" Marcus asked Tex trying to change the subject.

"Fine, we're just friends. I think she went out Jagger the other night."

"Seriously, just friends?"

"Yeah," Tex drawled as he worked on the white IKEA dresser in the corner. "I don't know how I do it, but I always end up in the friend zone."

"When the right one comes along, you won't have to worry about the friend zone. It'll just happen." Braxton responded.

"I'm going to get a beer, y'all want one?" Tex asked as he headed out of the room.

"Yeah," they both responded.

"Where's McKenzie and Emma?" Braxton turned back toward Marcus.

Emma really didn't have a lot of clothing, shoes or even some of the necessities she needs, so I handed her my credit card and sent them shopping," Marcus glanced over at Braxton, "I hope you have unlimited minutes and data on Kendall's phone. I have a feeling she will be shopping with them by way of the phone. McKenzie said she had a lot of questions for her."

"She probably will be. I was just thinking, I hope your credit card isn't unlimited," Braxton laughed. "Kendall's excited about being an aunt. She said she's going to spoil Emma. She said it'll be payback for you and McKenzie spoiling Jax and Josie."

"Oh great," Marcus chuckled.

"Did you really buy pink paint for this room?" Tex asked as he came back into the room carrying a bucket of paint and three beers.

"Emma said she wanted pink, it was her favorite color." Marcus laughed.

"You don't have to worry about us spoiling Emma, you're going to be the one to spoil her." Braxton chortled.

"Remind me again, what color is Josie's room?"

"It's pink, but it's light pink. This is Pepto Bismol pink."

"Emma picked it out." Marcus laughed and looked at the bucket with the paint sample color on top, "It really does look like Pepto Bismol pink," he shook his head. "Thanks, now that's all I'm going to think of when I walk in this room.

"Happy to help," Braxton smirked.

"McKenzie's painting a mural on the wall of a ballerina, maybe that will help tone the color down some." Marcus commented.

"It'll need to be a big ass mural to tone that pink down." Tex laughed.

"I might have to suggest that," Marcus shook his head.

"So, what's the plan with McKenzie and Emma once we head back to Atlanta. I mean we only have a week before we have to head back."

"Yeah, that's where the fun comes in." Marcus sighed.
"Emma will stay here with McKenzie. We are hiring a nanny to stay with Emma during the day while McKenzie goes into work. Whenever we have a few days in a row off, I'll fly down here. Basically, this is our home base. When it works with McKenzie's schedule, her and Emma will fly up to Atlanta or wherever we are playing," he paused and looked at his friends, "I'm also going to put my condo in Atlanta up for sale. I figured if it sales quickly, I could move in with one of you two bozos until the season is over.

"Which bozo is going to get your sorry ass?" Braxton asked.

"I'll let you fight over me," Marcus smirked. "You know you both want me."

"You're family, you get him," Tex looked over to Braxton with a smirk then glanced over to Marcus. "McKenzie's going to let you go off for six possibly seven months while she watches your kid?"

"Our kid," he corrected Tex. "Emma's already calling her Mama."

"Really?" Braxton and Tex said in unison.

"Yeah," Marcus chuckled at the response. "She feels weird about it, like she's disrespecting Holly or something, but Holly told her that's what she wanted. Emma needs a mom and Holly knew that. I think it's just going to take some time for her to not feel like she's being disrespectful. You can tell she loves Emma already and I really think she loves that she calls her Mama, she just feels guilty about it." He stopped to screw in another nut and bolt this time into a dresser. "Emma did call her mommy, but McKenzie told her to call her mama since Holly was mommy. She doesn't want to take that from her.

"I can understand that. It's got to be hard for McKenzie. The truth is, Emma is so young, McKenzie is going to be the only mom she's going to remember."

"I know, we're going to try and keep Holly's memory alive for Emma, but it's going to be hard since she had no family and I didn't really know her. She was a one-night stand, I didn't ask any questions, didn't want to know. I just wanted to get laid."

"Well those days are over," Braxton smiled. "Marriage and kids, it's a different world."

"I see that," Marcus looked around the room at the white wooden canopy bed they had just constructed. The white chiffon canopy with pink sparkles on top laid over the top of the bed. He glanced at it and knew McKenzie would have to help him get it situated on the bed in order to have the look she was going for. The white Ikea nightstands and dresser were ready to be pushed into place as well as the white desk.

"You know you are going to need to get anti-tip furniture straps for the dresser, right?" Braxton asked.

"Anti-tip what?" Marcus asked.

"Anti-tip furniture straps. They keep the dresser from tipping should Emma decide to climb it. Kendall made me put them on Josie's dressers."

"All these things I wouldn't even know to think about," Marcus shook his head. "I'm going to screw this up."

"No, you are not, it's a learn as you go process. You're already doing everything you can. Hell, you are painting an ugly ass pink wall in your house for her. She has you so tightly wrapped her finger. You are going to have one spoiled child. You better watch that." Braxton grinned.

"Yeah, you're one to talk. If Josie told you she wanted the Pepto Bismol pink in her room, she'd have it and let's not forget about Jax. Remind me again, who is the inspiration for the AAU baseball organization we are starting up once we officially retire."

"Okay, maybe you're right," Braxton chortled.

"Well I guess I'll run by the store after the game tonight and get the straps. We can put them in place after we paint tomorrow. I'll guess I'll push the dresser up against the wall where she can't climb the drawers or push it in the closet until we get it fixed."

Marcus glanced at Tex who was quiet and withdrawn at the moment. "What ya thinking about Tex?"

"Nothing much," he paused. "I'm happy for you guys. You both found the love of your lives, got kids and a family now. I have to admit, I'm a little jealous."

"You'll find the right girl one day. When you do, it'll hit out of the blue. You won't even be expecting it." Marcus smiled.

"We need to wrap this up," Tex changed the subject again, "we've got to be at practice in an hour."

"I think we've about got the furniture done," Marcus looked around the room. "Y'all coming back in the morning to help me paint?"

"Shouldn't we have painted before we put together the furniture?" Tex asked.

"Probably, but I wanted to go ahead and get her bed up. She's been sleeping in the bed between me and McKenzie. I'm ready to get her in her own bed. McKenzie and I need to practice for the honeymoon."

"Somehow I don't think you need practice," Braxton chuckled. "Might need practice in using a condom, but I think you got the sex part down."

"Ass," Marcus half-grinned. "Let's get this cleaned up and head to practice."

CHAPTER THIRTY

"Why the hell are we here at seven in the morning"" Tex asked as Marcus opened the front door.

"Because McKenzie's parents will be here for lunch to meet Emma and berate me, I'm sure." He stepped aside to let Tex in.

"Damn, it's early," Braxton commented as he walked up behind Tex.

"Thank you for helping," McKenzie came up holding two cups of coffee, handing one to Braxton and one to Tex.

"Thanks, little mama," Tex drawled as he leaned over and gave McKenzie a kiss on the cheek.

"Quit flirting with my woman," Marcus quirked.

"That ain't flirting," Tex commented. "This is," he wrapped one arm around McKenzie, pulled her in and gave her a kiss right smack on the lips. McKenzie took a step back shocked, but with a half-grin across her face.

"What the hell, Tex!"

"You better watch it, cowboy. You're going to get your ass kicked." Braxton shook his head.

"Nah, he's not going to kick my ass. At least not right now. He needs me to help paint those walls Pepto Bismol pink."

"On that note," McKenzie tried to divert their attention. "Are you guys hungry? I made you some breakfast before you got started painting."

"I definitely could eat," Tex grinned at her as he headed toward the kitchen.

"Me too," Braxton walked toward the kitchen then turned when he heard laughter coming from the living room.

"Emma is watching some cartoon about pink ponies or something." Marcus commented.

"I think it's hilarious you have a girl, after the way you paraded around with one woman after another," Braxton replied.

"Yeah, God definitely has a sense of humor," he shook his head, "She won't be allowed to date until she's thirty and even then, no baseball players."

"Okay, Mr. Harper," Braxton raised his brows.

"Shit! I did just sound like him, didn't I?"

"Yep. He told McKenzie no baseball players. That obviously didn't work out to well either." Braxton laughed. "Come on, I want to go meet my niece."

"Y'all sit down and eat. I'll get her, she needs to come in here and eat too.

Marcus headed into the living room to get Emma. A few minutes later she walked in the kitchen holding his hand. She stopped and looked when she saw Braxton and Tex standing at the kitchen bar looking in her direction.

"Who are they?" She stopped and looked up at her dad, stepping slightly behind him.

"Come here baby girl," he said pulling her in front and holding her hand. "I want you to meet my two best friends and your uncles." She nodded and grasped his hand a little tighter.

"Hi, I'm your Uncle Braxton," Braxton leaned down to the little girl and held out his hand. She took it, but then walked over to him and hugged him.

"Hi, Uncle Braxton. Do you have any kids?"

"Yes, I do," he chuckled. "I've got a little boy named Jax, we'll he's not so little anymore, he's ten. I've also got a little girl named Josie. They are your cousins and they can't wait to meet you. Your Aunt Kendall can't wait to meet you either."

"Who's Aunt Kendall?"

"She's my wife and McKenzie's, your mama's," Braxton corrected himself, "sister."

"Oh, well I can't wait to meet her too," she paused, "and my cousins." She then looked at Tex and walked over to him. "Who are you?"

"I'm Tex."

"Uncle Tex," Marcus corrected.

"Uncle Tex," he smiled.

Emma looked at him and then motioned for him to lean down with her finger. He leaned down until he was eye level with her. She put her hands around his neck and gave him a big hug. Tex smiled and wrapped his larger arms around her and then gave her a kiss on the top of her head.

"Hi Uncle Tex," she stepped back and put her small hands on his cheeks. "Do you have any kids?"

"No, I don't." He frowned.

"That's okay, I'll be your kid too. My daddy can share me with you."

"What?" Marcus belted out.

"You can share, right Daddy?" She looked at him with wide eyes, "it's polite to share.

"I'm not sure I want to share my daughter," he muttered, "or my wife," he looked at Tex who laughed aloud.

"Okay, let's eat, so we can get that room painted before Mommy and Daddy Dearest get here," Braxton commented.

"Hey, that's my parents your talking about." McKenzie glanced at Braxton.

"And my in-laws, so I get to make those jokes," he smiled and then stuffed his mouth with a fork full of eggs.

◆ ◆ ◆

"Daddy, I love my room! Thank you! Thank you! Thank you!" Emma shouted as she danced around the room.

"Glad you like little bit," he smiled as she came up and gave him a big hug.

"Where's my hug, I helped paint and put the room together," Tex inquired.

"Thank you, Uncle Tex," Emma ran to him and wrapped his arms around him."

"Um,hm," Braxton cleared his throat.

"Thank you, Uncle Braxton," she let go of Tex and went to hug Braxton.

"The bright pink isn't as bad with all the white furniture and once I get the mural up, that should help tone it down too." McKenzie commented looking around the room.

"You were worried about the bright pink too?" Marcus asked looking at her.

"Yeah, but it's what Emma wanted, so I wasn't going to say anything," she smiled as she grabbed the light pink sheets and began putting them on the bed.

Just as she tucked in onside of the fitted sheet the doorbell rang.

"Looks like Mommy and Daddy Dearest are here," Braxton commented.

"Marcus, can you go get that? I'm kind of pre-occupied right now."

"I can think of a better way to pre-occupy you," Marcus smirked as the doorbell rang again.

"Marcus," McKenzie sighed.

"Braxton, you go get the door. I don't want to face Daddy Dearest yet." Marcus. Looked to his soon to be brother-in-law.

"No way, it's not my house. You go get they're door. There here to interrogate you, not me."

"That's what I'm afraid of," Marcus grimaced as the doorbell rang for the third time.

"I'll go get the door. I'm not fucking one of his daughters, so I should be safe."

"Tex!" Marcus, McKenzie and Braxton all yelled at the same time.

"What?"

"Language, little ears," Marcus commented as he looked over to Emma who was engrossed in trying to help McKenzie make her bed.

"Shit, didn't think about that," Tex said, "Shit, did it again," he paused and rolled his eyes. "Crap, I'm getting the door before I say something else."

"We need your mom Braxton," Marcus commented. "She's the lonely one I know that can reign in Tex' language."

"True, but even she can only manage so much," Braxton chortled.

"I can't wait until he has kids. I'm interested to

see how much he tones down his language then," Marcus laughed.

"Come on let's go. We can't leave Tex alone with my parents too long." McKenzie remarked as she put the finishing touches on Emma's bed.

McKenzie took Emma's hand and headed out of the room followed closely by Marcus and Braxton. As she entered the living room, Mr. Harper and Tex were standing in the kitchen drinking a beer and talking. Mrs. Harper was sitting on the sofa messing with some packages. She looked up and her eyes widened as she saw McKenzie and Emma walk into the room.

"Hey Mom, Hey Dad," McKenzie remarked.

"Well if it isn't my daughter, my son-in-law and the pain in my ass," Mr. Harper announced.

"Dad!" McKenzie put her hands over Emma's ears.

"Good to see you too Mr. Harper." Marcus sarcastically remarked.

"Bill! Behave yourself," Mrs. Harper scolded him.

"I thought I told you to keep your catcher away from my daughter." Mr. Harper scowled as he looked over to Braxton.

"Hey, there is only so much I can do," he shook his head. "You didn't do such a good job of keeping your daughter away from my catcher."

"She's hard-headed."

"So, is he."

"Boys!" Mrs. Harper broke in. "Behave," she sighed. "Now, let me meet my new granddaughter to be," Mrs. Harper walked over to Emma and squatted in front of her until she was eye level with her. "Hey, Emma, I'm going to be your new grandmother really soon. As soon as your daddy and McKenzie get married. You can call me Nana, that's what your cousins call me."

Emma smiled a weak smile and then turned and looked at McKenzie. She leaned down to look Emma in the eyes. "Emma, this is my mom. She's going to be your nana and this," McKenzie holds her hand out motioning for her dad to come over, "is my dad," she says as he comes of and takes her hand. "He's going to be your new papi."

"Who came up with Papi?" Tex asked.

"It was something Jax came up with when he was little, now all the grandkids call him that." Mrs. Harper smiled then looked back to Emma. "Papi and I brought some presents for you. Do you want to open them?" she asked as she put her hand out to Emma.

"Yes!" Emma's eyes got wide and she took her hand.

Mrs. Harper lead Emma to the sofa where the presents were laid out.

"Good grief, Mom," McKenzie began, "you'd think it's Christmas." She took in all the bags sitting on the coffee table.

"It's not every day I get a new granddaughter." She smiled as she sat down on the sofa and pulled Emma next to her, handing her a package. "We just need a wedding now."

"If Dad doesn't run Marcus off," McKenzie replied.

"Oh, they'll be a wedding. Even if it's a shotgun wedding. He's given me a granddaughter now, so he's got marry my daughter." Mr. Harper commented.

"I'm marrying your daughter, you can keep your shotgun." Marcus paused and looked at him. "You are one crazy ass bastard, first you tell me to stay away from your daughter, then your threatening me with a shotgun if I don't marry her."

"Welcome to the family," Braxton grinned.

"Marcus, language," McKenzie scolded him.

"Uh, I've got to work on that," Marcus grimaced.

"Well, you've given me a granddaughter now. Guess I'm stuck with your ass," Mr. Harper responded.

"Bill, language," Mrs. Harper mimicked McKenzie.

"Besides," he looked at him, "you're going to find she's just like her mother, hard-headed, stubborn and will get on to you about everything, like your language," Mr. Harper cracked a smile as Mrs. Harper stared him down with an evil look telling him he was in trouble later. "You dug your own grave, son." He smiled and patted him on the back.

"You two done?" McKenzie asked.

"For now," Marcus remarked as he went and sat beside Emma. "What did you get squirt?"

Emma excitedly showed him all the things McKenzie parents had brought from clothing and shoes to dolls, dress-up clothes and coloring books. She was so excited about it all. Marcus figured, based on what he had seen in California and what she brought with her, it was the most she had received at one time during her short life.

CHAPTER THIRTY-ONE

"You sure you just want to go to the court house and get married. You don't a big wedding?" Mrs. Harper asked as she sliced tomatoes for the burgers.

"Yeah, Mom," Kendall is flying down with the kids on Friday to see the final game of spring training. They'll be here for the weekend and ride back with Braxton. We are going to do a wedding reception, well barbeque, at Braxton's on Saturday. It'll be fun. Then everyone can head back on Sunday for the first game of the season Monday night." McKenzie replied.
"Everyone will head back, including your husband and you'll be left here with Emma," her mother stated.

"Mom, don't go there please," McKenzie sighed. "He's retiring at the end of this year, it's only one season."

"I know, but it'll be tough as a newlywed and instance mom."

"I know, but we'll be fine. We've been through a lot worse."

"I know you have," Mrs. Harper responded, "and I see how much you love each other. It's just going be tough."

"I know," McKenzie sliced into an onion, "but we will still see each other throughout the season. He'll come home when he can, and Emma and I will travel to him when we can. In fact, we are heading to Atlanta with everyone else on Sunday. We'll fly home Thursday when the team heads out to Cincinnati. Piper is going to pick me and Emma up at the airport."

"Good, at least you are getting to spend your first week as husband and wife together."

"Yeah, we'll be fine Mom. Don't worry about us."

"I'm your Mom, I'm going to worry," Mrs. Harper turned to make the tea, "just make sure you don't get pregnant until the season is over. You don't want to go through that alone and try to take care of a child."

"Yes, Mom. You gonna give Marcus the condom talk, like Dad did?" McKenzie chuckled.

"No, I'm gonna give you the birth control speech," she replied. "It's your responsibility as much as it is his. Make sure you take care of it now if you haven't already done so. Then you and Marcus can decide together when it is time to give Emma a sibling and me more grandkids."

"Yes, Mom," McKenzie pulled apart the lettuce and placed it on the plate, knowing she could very well be pregnant. The last several times they had sex, protection was not a priority.

"Burgers and hot dogs are done, Everything ready in here?" Mr. Harper asked bringing in a plate full of meat. Braxton and Tex followed behind him, with Marcus trailing, carrying Emma on his back. He had to duck in the doorway to keep from hitting her head.

"Papi made me a hotdog and a hamburger!" Emma told McKenzie.

"Wow! That was nice of him, wasn't it?" McKenzie smiled.

"Un, huh?" she nodded with a big grin on her face.

"Think you can eat that much squirt?" Tex asked.

"Ummm," she looked like she was thinking, then stopped and looked at him in all seriousness. "I'll eat some, and you can eat the rest."

"Oh, great! Slobber burgers, my favorite," Tex laughed. "You know what munchkin," Tex lifted her off Marcus's shoulder and sat her down looking her in her eye. "Your dad told me, he wanted to eat what you didn't finish. You make sure you give it to him, okay. We don't want to hurt his feelings," he winked.

"Okay!" Emma smiled and then ran to get her doll.

"Thanks a lot man," Marcus commented.

"Hey, man, that's part your DNA. If anyone gets the slobber burger, it's you."

"Yum, can't wait." Marcus laughed.

"Bull, get over here," Mr. Harper hollered looking at Marcus.

"Did he just call me Bull?" he glanced at Tex.

"I believe he did."

"Bull, as in bullshit?"

"I'm thinking Bull as in the animal?"

"Why?"

"Because Bulls are only good for breeding and bull riding."

"Shit, that's great," Marcus shook his head as he walked toward Mr. Harper, "Bull, really?"

"Yeah, they are only good for one thing, breeding, just like you," Mr. Harper grabbed a beer.

"Even, I don't have a nickname," Braxton laughed.

"Hey, pretty boy, take your mother-in-law an iced tea." Mr. Harper handed a glass to Braxton.

"Pretty boy, great," Braxton shook his head,

"Thanks, Marcus."

"Cowboy, grab the buns," Mr. Harper shouted orders to Tex.

"Oh, look, I get a nickname too. I feel like part of the family now," Tex put his hands over his heart. "Got any more daughters, Mr. Harper."

"Nope, but McKenzie's not married yet. She's still fair game and seems to like baseball players."

"Hey," Marcus chimed in, "she's mine, hands off."

"I don't know Marcus," Tex walked over to McKenzie and put his arms around her, "What ya say McKenzie? You. Me. A romantic walk in the moonlight."

"You know Tex," McKenzie winked, "if anything ever happens to Marcus, you're my man."

"Hands off my woman," Marcus lifted Tex' hand from McKenzie's shoulder and quickly dropped it as he pulled her into him.

"Jealous much?" McKenzie leaned over and kissed Marcus on the cheek.

"Only when other men are touching you," he pulled her in closer. "Saturday, you will officially be all mine."

"Jealousy doesn't become you baby," she planted a quick kiss on his lips.

"Oh, quit your yapping over there," Mr. Harper grunted, "We're out of beer, Bull, got any more?"

"There is more in the garage, I'll go get it," he glanced toward the kitchen. "We've gone through them faster than I expected."

"Why's that? You got a drinking problem, Bull?"

"No, sir, I don't. In fact, I've only had one today." Although I may have four or five more before you leave, he mumbled to himself as he walked toward the garage.

"Marcus, "Mrs. Harper followed Marcus into the garage.

"Don't let him get to you," she put her hand on his shoulder. "He'll back off once you and McKenzie are married. He did the same with Braxton."

"I don't recall him and Braxton having this much trouble."

"They did, but not to the extreme. I think he was just happy to have Jax's father in his life, so he didn't really want to run him off."

"Is that what he is trying to do to me, run me off?"

"He's testing to you to see if you will run."

"So, why are you telling me, don't you want to know if I'm going to run too?"

"You're not. I've seen you with McKenzie and you two have been through hell and back together. You're not going to let her dad run you off."

"That's true, I'm not going anywhere."

"Besides, I'm not going to let him run you off, because if you go, my new granddaughter goes and I'm not letting that happen."

"Thank you," Marcus leaned over and kissed Mrs. Harper on the top of her head.

"For what?"

"For accepting Emma as one of your own."

"As far as I am concerned, she is one of mine and no one is going to tell me different." She gave him a quick hug and then returned back into the house as Marcus headed to the outdoor refrigerator to grab more beer.

CHAPTER THIRTY-TWO

Saturday morning came, Marcus and McKenzie were awaken to a little girl jumping in the bed.

"Wake-up, wake-up, sleepy heads," Emma sang as she jumped on the bed.

"Sleepy heads, huh?" Marcus grabbed her and pulled her down tickling her making her giggle.

"Uh," McKenzie moaned as she jumped up and ran to the toilet.

"Emma, go play with your dolls. I'll be there in a minute and we can make breakfast together." Marcus lifted Emma up and then sat her on the ground watching her run out of the room.

"Kenz, you okay?" Marcus asked as he slowly walked into the bathroom.

McKenzie was leaning over the toilet bowl dry heaving. Marcus rushed over and pulled her hair back until she finally sat back on her knees.

"You okay?" Marcus grabbed a wash cloth and ran it under some water. He rung it out, folded it, then laid it across the back of her neck.

"Yeah, I don't know what happened. The bed started moving and I started feeling sick to my stomach.

"You're not nervous about anything are you? Like marrying me today?" Marcus bit his lip.

"No, I promise you, I'm not nervous about marrying you at all. Being with you feels natural, you know.

It just feels right. I can't wait to become Mrs. Marcus Hunter. You have nothing to worry about there." She took the wet wash cloth off her neck and washed her face with it. "I've actually been feeling kind of nauseated the past couple of days. I really hope I'm not coming down with something."

Marcus stood back and looked at McKenzie in deep thought, "McKenzie, have you had your period since the miscarriage?"

"No, but the doctor said it could take six weeks before it came back."

"Can you get pregnant during those six weeks?"

"I don't know, I was so distraught at the time, I didn't think to ask," she paused and looked at Marcus. "You don't think I'm pregnant, do you?"

"We'll your dad did nickname me Bull," Marcus half-grinned.

"Crap," McKenzie buried her hands, "I don't want to be pregnant, not yet."

"Listen, I know you wanted to get further along in your career before having any more kids, but if you are pregnant, I'll be retired by the time the baby is born. I'll take care of it while you go to work."

"It's not that," she glanced at him with tears welding in her eyes, "I'm going to be alone throughout the pregnancy. You're going to be traveling all over the states playing ball and I'll be hear getting bigger and bigger by myself and no one to hold my hair while I puke or run to the grocery store late at night to get me rocky road ice cream to curve my cravings."

"Is that what you craved with the first pregnancy?"

"Yes," she sat with her back against the tub, pulling her knees up, she buried her faced in her knees and began to sob.

"Oh, baby," Marcus sat beside her, wrapped his arm around her shoulder and pulled her in, "I'm sorry I wasn't there, but this time will be different, I promise. I will be down here every break I get. If there is enough time between games, I'll even fly down just for the night. When I'm here I will stock up with all the rocky road ice cream and anything else you are craving. We can put it in the freezer in the garage."

"Okay," McKenzie tried to pull it together.

"Besides, we don't know if that's what it is or not, it could just be a stomach bug," he leaned over and kissed her temple, "but I'm not going to lie, I'll be ecstatic if you are pregnant. I would see it as God giving us another chance."

"Yeah," McKenzie half grinned.

Marcus pulled his arm from her shoulder, stood up and took McKenzie hands pulling her up.

"Let's go make some breakfast and get ready to head to the court house. Afterwards we can stop by the drug store and get a test."

"Okay."

"And baby, if you are pregnant, I'll consider it the best wedding present I could have gotten."

"Shit! I didn't get you a wedding present!" McKenzie suddenly realized.

"I didn't get you one either, so we're good." Marcus smiled. "We've kind of had a lot going on."

"True," she mumbled as she began brushing her teeth.

"Kenz, are you really okay, with going to the

court house. I'm not depriving you of some big wedding you want, am I," he paused for a moment. "I mean, if your wanting a big wedding we can hold off."

"Marcus Hunter, are you trying to get out of marrying me?" McKenzie asked as she spit the toothpaste out.

"Hell, no," he smirked. "I'm ready to marry you now. I just don't want you to regret not having a big wedding."

"I just want to marry you," she kissed his lips tenderly. "I don't care about all the hoopla. I just want to be married to you."

"Daddy, Mama, I'm hungry," Emma came running into the bathroom carrying two dolls, one under each hand.

"I don't know if I'll ever get used to being called Mama."

"I know, it's crazy, right?" Marcus lifted Emma up and held her with his left arm and then grabbed McKenzie's hand with his free hand, "let's go make breakfast.

Marcus and McKenzie stood in front of the judge, family and friends reciting their vows. Kendall and the kids had flown down to be there as well as Marcus' mother. Braxton stood with Kendall, Jax and Josie, while Mr. and Mrs. Harper stood off to the side with Mrs. Hunter. Tex stood near Braxton and Kendall holding Emma in his arms watching on.

As soon as the wedding vows were completed,

Marcus took Emma's hand and they walked over to the table. The judged signed the adoption papers officially making McKenzie Emma's mother. Emma was so excited, she began to twirl around in her new pink dress that McKenzie had bought her for the special day.

"Your dad and I got you something," McKenzie pulled a small bag out of her purse and then leaned down to look Emma in the eye. "Today, you dad and I got rings to show everyone we are a family. We wanted to get you something special too, so that we could show everyone that we are now a family." Today was about much more than McKenzie becoming Mrs. Marcus Hunter, it was about them all becoming a family.

"What ya get me?" Emma asked excitedly as she took the bag. She opened the bag and pulled out a pretty platinum gold chain necklace with a heart locket. In the middle of the locket was a pink topaz.

"Open the heart," McKenzie smiled.

Emma opened the locket and on each side was a picture. On the right was a picture of Marcus and Emma and on the left was a picture of Marcus, McKenzie and Emma. Emma was so excited, she grabbed the necklace and held it up to McKenzie, jumping up and down.

"Put it on me! Put it on me! Please," she begged.

"Okay, okay," McKenzie laughed as she took the necklace from Emma's hand. "Stay still for a minute while I put it on," she commanded as Emma quit jumping.

Marcus leaned down next to McKenzie, gave her a quick kiss on the lips, then took Emma's long dark blonde hair an pulled it up so McKenzie could put the necklace on. After McKenzie put it on and double checked it, Emma ran to Mr. and Mrs. Harper.

"Look what Daddy and Mama gave me," she took her little hand on the necklace and showed it to them.

"It's so weird hearing anyone call McKenzie Mama," Mrs. Harper looked at Mr. Harper.

"Yeah, it is," he responded.

"Let me see your pretty necklace," Mrs. Harper said as she leaned down and looked at the necklace. "It's so pretty, your daddy and mama must love you very much."

"They do!" Emma squeaked and then ran over and wrapped one arm around Marcus' leg and one arm around McKenzie's leg and squeezed tight.

"Okay, the family dynamics have changed since our last family picture. I want a family picture before we leave here." Mrs. Harper demanded.

"We can go outside to the park and I'll take the picture for you," Tex suggested.

"That sounds good, but I want a picture with you in it too. Your Uncle Tex to all my grandkids, which makes you family too."

"Thank you, Ma'am. These guys are definitely family to me." Tex responded.

"Come on, let's go get me that family picture. We can get someone at the park to take the picture." Mrs. Harper took Emma's hand and headed out the door, followed closely by Braxton and his family, Tex, and Marcus with his arm wrapped around McKenzie.

"Come on wife, our first official family picture awaits us." He pulled her in to him and laid a passionate kiss on her before following the others out the

Christy Ryan

door.

CHAPTER THIRTY-THREE

After making a stop by the pharmacy to pick up a pregnancy test, the Hunters made it to the neighborhood park where Braxton and Tex had started up the grill. Marcus' family, friends and teammates as well as McKenzie's family, friends and some of her co-workers had arrived to help them celebrate their nuptials.

"About time y'all got here," Tex drawled.

"We had to make a quick stop on the way," Marcus replied as he walked toward the guys.   McKenzie took off and headed over toward Kendall as Emma ran off to the playground.

"Need some things for the honeymoon?" Braxton teased.

"As a matter of fact," Marcus smirked.

"Kendall said Emma is staying with us tonight, so you two could have a honeymoon night," Braxton remarked.

"Yeah, I think McKenzie and Kendall sat that up."

"I still can't believe Marcus Hunter is married with a kid," Tex commented as he flipped the burgers.

"I can't believe it either," Marcus paused, "at least the kid part." He grabbed a beer, popped it open and looked over at McKenzie. "I knew Kenz was it for me the moment I saw her."

"It took you a while to do anything about it," Braxton sipped his beer.

"Yeah, I don't know why. I never had a problem

making a move before, but then again, I never wanted more than a one-night stand before McKenzie."

"Well, it was a good thing you finally asked her out. I was about to make my move and we all know once you have Tex, you'll never go back."

"Shut up, Tex," Marcus rolled his eyes.

"Where is that wife of yours? I need to give her a congratulatory kiss."

"No!" Marcus decreed, "you can keep your hands and any other part of you off of her. I've officially made her mine."

"Ehh, she's still free game. The marriage can still be annulled, you haven't had time to consummate it yet." Tex continued to tease Marcus.

"We stopped by the pharmacy for a pregnancy test on the way here." Marcus confessed.

"What!" Braxton and Tex shouted in unison.

"You didn't see fit to use the condoms Coach passed out?" Braxton asked.

"I think it was already too late by that point."

"I guess you did earn the name Bull," Tex chuckled.

"Shit, Mr. Harper and Coach are going to kill you." Braxton commented.

"At least, I can say it's my wife who is pregnant this time, not my girlfriend or some one-night stand."

"Somehow, I still think you're going to catch shit from it." Tex drawled.

"Yep, probably," Marcus remarked as a few of his teammates headed his way.

"Hey man, can't believe Marcus Hunter finally tied the knot," Jacob held his hand out, Marcus took it and shook it.

"Yeah, I figured it was about time I made an honest woman out of her," Marcus laughed.

"More of her making an honest man out of you," Xander chimed in, "Congratulations man."

"Thanks, man."

"It took you long enough to ask her out. I was going to ask her out if you didn't hurry and make your move." Niko patted him on his shoulder.

"She's not into your kinky stuff, Niko," Marcus chortled. "It wouldn't have worked."

"How do know? Have you ever tried get kinky with her? She might surprise you," Niko smirked. "Most woman aren't as vanilla as they seem."

"Shut the hell up, Niko," Marcus chuckled. "Go find yourself another woman."

"I was thinking Sawyer's mom. Have you seen her?" Niko wiggled his eyes.

"Stay the hell away from my mother," Sawyer ordered as he came up. "She's off limits," Sawyer looked at Niko and then at all his teammates, "to all of you."

"Dude, your mom's hot!" Xander spoke up.

"She's my mother. Same rules apply to teammates mothers that apply to the girlfriends."

"You mean hands off another man's woman rule?" Tex asked.

"Yeah," Sawyer nodded.

"Not everyone follows that rule," Marcus snorted, "Tex crossed the line a few times with McKenzie."

Tex laughed and then took a big gulp of his beer grinning from ear to ear.

"Dude, I don't remember anything about mother's being in that rule." Xander responded.

"That's because most mothers aren't as hot as Sawyer's mother," Niko smirked, "of course, that means there's no rule."

"Oh, there's a rule," Sawyer's eyes narrowed. "It's called Stay the Fuck Away From my Mother."

"Y'all leave the poor kid alone," Marcus laughed. "Go get everyone. It's time to eat."

Just as some of the guys went off to gather everyone together, Mr. Harper walked up to Marcus.

"Marcus."

"Mr. Harper."

"Listen, I know I've been tough on you this past year and even more so recently." Mr. Harper began.

"Tough is kind of an understatement."

"Yeah, I know," he began, "I should apologize, but I'm not. I wanted to make sure you were good enough for my daughter."

"Is anyone good enough for your daughter?"

"No," Mr. Harper paused, "but you've proven that you are worthy of her. It's obvious how much you love her and how much she loves you," he paused again. "I guess what I am trying to say, is welcome to the family." Mr. Harper held out his hand.

"Thanks," Marcus took Mr. Harper's hand and shook it.

"I want you to know, as far as I'm concerned, Emma is one of ours, just like Jax and Josie. I've already gotten attached to that little girl."

"Thank you, Mr. Harper, that means a lot."

"That also doesn't mean, I'm going to get off your back or quit giving you shit."

"I wouldn't expect any less." Marcus commented as Mr. Harper nodded his head and then headed off toward his wife.

"Guess your officially part of the family now," Braxton commented as they watched Mr. Harper walk off.

"Yeah, who would have thought you and I would have actually ended up brothers-in-law?"

"Couldn't have asked for a better brother-in-law," Braxton smiled.

"Thanks, man," Marcus grinned. "Now let's feed this hungry group of people."

CHAPTER THIRTY-FOUR

McKenzie walked down the hall and sat down on the sofa. Marcus sat on the floor next to Emma. She had him coloring in her Barbie Ballerina Coloring Book. McKenzie chuckled at how that little girl who just came into their lives had Marcus wrapped around her little finger.

"So?" Marcus looked up as McKenzie sat down.

"We wait five minutes," she responded.

"Are you going to be okay, whichever way this goes?" Marcus laid the crayon down on the table. Kissed Emma on the head and then sat down next to McKenzie.

"Yeah," she sighed, "I'm just scared about doing this by myself, if this is positive. Because let's face it, you'll be traveling most of the time."

"I know, and I've thought about retiring before my contract was fulfilled, but we lose a lot of money if I do."

"I know," McKenzie half grinned. "I'll be okay."

"If you are," he took her hand, "we are going to make it work. I swear the airlines will know me by name."

"They already do," she forced a grin.

"True, but I'll have my own personal seat, I'll be on the plane so much."

"I know, we've talked about this over and over again," she leaned over and kissed him, "I know you will do everything you can."

"What time is Kendall supposed to be here to get Emma?" Marcus looked at his daughter.

"Any minute now," she was going to run by the grocery store while Braxton and Tex cleaned up the stuff from the Barbeque, reception, whatever it was." McKenzie announced just as the doorbell rang. "Speaking of," she got up to answer the door.

"Aunt Kin Kin," Emma jumped and ran to the door.

"Hey princess," Kendall leaned down and gave her a hug. "You ready to play with Jax and Josie?"

"Yes!" Emma started out the door.

"Wait a minute," McKenzie caught her as she headed out, "Don't Daddy and I get a good-bye hug and kiss?"

"Okay," she came back kissed McKenzie, who was squatting, on the cheek. "Bye Mama," and then ran over to Marcus. "Bye, Daddy."

"Bye Princess," Marcus said as he picked her up and gave her a big hug and kiss. He handed her overnight bag to Kendall and watched them as they headed out the door. "Time to check," he turned back to McKenzie.

"Yeah," McKenzie sighed. "It's been more than five minutes."

Marcus took her hand and led her back to the bedroom. When they got to the room, he started walking toward the bathroom door, but McKenzie froze.

"Baby, it's going to be okay. Whatever happens, happens," Marcus tried to reassure her.

"I know. The truth is, I don't know what I want. If it says I'm positive, I'll be happy, but scared off doing it alone. Then again if it's negative, I'll be disappointed."

"So, it sounds like, either way you want this child, you just don't want to be alone."

"Yeah."

"You know if I'll do whatever I can. I would even retire without fulfilling my contract if you really want that, but Kenz, that's several million dollars we lose."

"I know, and I won't ask you to do that," she paused, "you'll just have to cater to my every whim the next child."

"That's a deal, I promise," he leaned over and kissed her then took her hand and lead her into the bathroom. He walked over and picked up the tests and looked at it, then looked at McKenzie with his eye brows raised and a confused look on his face. "What am I looking for?"

"One line means negative; two lines mean positive."

"So, two pink lines, mean...."

"We're having a baby," McKenzie interrupted.

Marcus picked McKenzie up and spun her around and then began kissing her all over her face. He then began nibbling at her ear, then grabbed her legs and wrapped them around his waist walking her into the bedroom. He gently laid her on the bed and then began to crawl up on the bed, when the doorbell rang.

"Ugh," Marcus groaned. "Maybe if we ignore it, they'll go away."

"Go check, it could be Kendall, Emma might have forgotten something."

"Ugh, okay, I'll go check Mama," Marcus leaned

over and kissed her forehead and then stood up adjusting himself. "If it's Kendall, she may get more of an eyeful then she wants."

"Just go," McKenzie chuckled. "Pull your shirt over your pants."

Marcus pulled his shirt out and let it hang lose over his pants as not to show whoever was at the door his growing bulge. He mumbled all the way to the door and groaned when he opened the door to see Tex standing there.

"Hey, not wanting to disrupt the honeymoon," he chortled looking at Marcus, "but I volunteered to bring the wedding gifts over while Braxton and Jagger ran the leftover food to the homeless shelter." Tex walked over to the kitchen table and laid down several bags full of gifts.

"Oh, whatever, you know you wanted to interrupt us." Marcus snorted.

"Okay, you got me," Tex smirked. "I volunteered to bring the gifts over. I figured you haven't consummated the marriage yet, I still have a chance," he teased. "Looks like I got here just in time."

"She's pregnant." Marcus commented.

"For sure?" Tex asked.

"Yep, we just took the test."

"Well, damn, guess I got find another woman now."

"You always had to find another woman."

"Congratulations, man. I mean that," Tex held out his hand. "We all knew you and McKenzie belonged together, it just took you long enough to get there."

"Thanks."

"Doesn't mean, I won't still hit on her," Tex winked as McKenzie walked into the room. "Well, darlin'. I hear congratulations are in order."

"You told him?" She looked at Marcus.

"He's still trying to pick you up." Marcus commented. "Even on the night of the wedding."

"Aw, Tex," McKenzie came up and gave him a hug, "you know if I ever get tired of Marcus…"

"Hey," Marcus chimed in.

"I'm going to let you two go and enjoy your wedding night," Tex opened the fridge to grab a beer. "You might want to check out Niko's gift, I hear he gives interesting gifts."

"Think there are any handcuffs in there?" Marcus walked toward the table of gifts.

"Aww, honey, you want me to handcuff you to the bed?" McKenzie grinned.

"No, I was thinking, I'd handcuff you."

"On that note," Tex said just as his phone rang. "Hello."

"Hey Mom, What's up?"

"What?"

"Okay, listen, I'm not at home. I'll call you later, just have Josh take over for Dad and hire a ranch hand to help him."

"I know you don't have the money, I'll take care of it."

"Okay, just take care of that and I'll call you back later."

"Everything okay?" McKenzie walked over and put her hand on Tex' shoulder.

"My Dad has lung cancer. He's been doing chemotherapy and fighting it, but all the radiation is making him weaker. He can't run the farm right now. He went out today and tried to help but collapsed. That's what Mom was calling about."

"Why didn't you tell us this Tex?" Marcus asked. "You, me and Braxton, we've always told each other everything."

"I know man, it's just with everything going on lately, I just didn't want to bring it up. It just always seemed like something was going on, Kendall and the kidnapping, McKenzie and the baby and then Emma..." Tex trailed off.

"This has been going on since back when Kendall was kidnapped?" McKenzie asked wrapping her arm around Tex and pulling him toward the couch."

"Yes, Josh, our foreman, has been doing Dad's job and his, but it's just getting to be too much for him. Which I'm sure is why Dad was out there helping."

"Is there anything we can do?" Marcus asked.

"Nah, I think if Josh takes over and we hire a ranch hand to help him, that will keep things running. Once the baseball season is over, I'll head back to Texas and help Josh," he paused. "Hell, my contract is up this year like yours and Braxton's, maybe it's time for me to retire too. Go back home, run the ranch."

"Look, don't rush into any decisions. You've got the season to figure things out. Maybe with the new ranch hand things will improve. Remember you're not in this alone, we may not be blood related, but you, me and Braxton, we are brothers till the end and we will be there for you." Marcus paused., "hell, Maybe Braxton and I can bring the wives and kids down and help out some."

"Fuck man, what do you and Braxton know about

running a ranch?" He laughed, "besides, you're going to need to be worrying about your pregnant wife and brand-new baby, not me."

"We'll make it work, we're there for you man." Marcus grinned.

"Thanks man," I'm leaving now so you can enjoy your wife and the new toys Niko got you, you've only got tonight and then it's toff o Atlanta and your final season in baseball and possibly mine." Tex stood up and walked out the door before they could say anything else.

"Well wife," Marcus stood and held out his hand to McKenzie. "Let's go consummate this marriage."

"Oh, so romantic," McKenzie sarcastically replied as she stood and took Marcus' hand and he led her off to their room and the beginning of their new life together as husband and wife.

OTHER BOOKS BY CHRISTY RYAN

A Baseball Romance Series

Game Changer
(Book 1)

Tex
(Book 3_
Release Date expected Juner2019

Stolen Innocence
Release Date expected March 2019

Remain Silent Series

Remain Silent
The first in a series of Heroes books
Release Date expected January 2020

50203888R00131

Made in the USA
Columbia, SC
04 February 2019